THE LAST SECRET

Robert Jackson

CHAPTER ONE

Before the outbreak of war in September 1939, Wesel had been an unremarkable though attractive little town, sitting astride the main road that crossed the Rhine on its way from Venlo, on the Dutch border, to Münster. In the five and a half years since then it had been fortunate enough to remain unremarkable, having escaped the attentions of the waves of Allied bombers that had systematically pounded the industrial cities of the Third Reich to rubble by night and day.

In February 1945, with the Reich tottering towards defeat, the twenty-five thousand civilian inhabitants of Wesel suddenly found their numbers swollen beyond all counting by masses of German troops, driven across the Rhine by the relentless Allied onslaught from the west together with what remained of their tanks, artillery and motor vehicles.

They were the cause of Wesel's eventual martyrdom.

It began on the sixteenth of February, when a hundred Lancaster bombers of the Royal Air Force, surrounded by swarms of escorting fighters, thundered over the little town and carpeted it from end to end with high explosive. When the bombers departed, six hundred of Wesel's civilian inhabitants lay dead in the ruins. Before nightfall on that day the German Army commander in the area, knowing what was to come, gave orders for the civilian population to be evacuated.

The evacuation was still in progress on the next day, when no fewer than three hundred heavy bombers bore down on Wesel. The dazed people headed for their shelters and prayed for a miracle.

It happened. Wesel was covered by cloud, and the raid was called off after only eight Halifaxes had dropped their bombs.

The sheltering clouds hung over Wesel for a fortnight, so that by the time the town was visited by fifty Mosquitos on the sixth of March less than two thousand of its original inhabitants remained. Each day they looked fearfully towards the north-western sky, and as the days passed they almost came to believe that the miracle still held. For fifteen days the Royal Air Force left Wesel alone.

On the sixteenth day, March the twenty-third, the bombers came again. Between dusk and the early hours of the following morning, three hundred Halifaxes and Lancasters unloaded eighteen hundred tons of bombs onto the hapless town.

Daylight, struggling through a great pall of dust and smoke, revealed that Wesel had ceased to exist. In its place was a lunar landscape where huge craters overlapped one another. Here and there, fragments of shattered buildings poked up amid forests of splintered tree trunks. In the centre of the town a devastated church, its fallen masonry centuries old, stood in isolation. A few hours earlier, shops and homes had clustered around it; now they were levelled into a wasteland of rubble.

Before the dust from the last sticks of bombs began to settle, a great airborne armada descended on Wesel and the surrounding countryside. It consisted of seventeen hundred aircraft, nearly fourteen hundred of which were towing gliders. The remainder, in the first wave, were laden with paratroops.

The British element of the armada had taken off from airfields in East Anglia in the pre-dawn twilight, crossing the Channel coast to the south of Calais. The American element, by far the larger of the two, had taken off a little later from the great cluster of airfields around Paris, most of them temporary strips laid down in support of the Allied advance across the continent.

Over the Belgian town of Wavre the two elements joined forces, forming a single great phalanx of aircraft bearing nearly twenty-two thousand men into battle. The recently liberated Belgians looked up from their towns and villages in awe and wonder, deafened by the sound of engines as column after column of glider-towing transports thundered overhead, heading inexorably towards the Rhine and the German frontier.

To the west of Wesel, British commandos were already slipping across the Rhine in inflatable boats, their task to destroy enemy artillery positions and sow confusion in the German defences prior to the full-scale assault of Field Marshal Bernard Montgomery's 21st Army Group. That would come first; the task of the British and American airborne forces was to capture and hold the wooded stretch of hills that formed the western edge of the Diersfordter Wald, a strategic position that would dominate the battle area.

Beyond the woods, nearer by some miles to the interior of Germany, ran the River Issel. It was crossed by three bridges — two road and one railway — and to capture and hold them was a primary objective of the British 6th and American 17th Airborne Divisions. The seizure of these bridges would mean that the path to the heart of Western Germany, and beyond, to Berlin itself, would lie open.

By 9.45 a.m. the great airborne fleet was approaching its objectives. From the cockpits of the transports, the crews could see the broad silver streak of the Rhine. Beyond it, the far bank was obscured by a thick black haze, the clouds of smoke and dust thrown up by the bombing of Wesel.

Ahead of the Armada, the Typhoons and Tempests of the RAF and the Mustangs and Thunderbolts of the USAAF screamed down through the smoke to pulverize enemy flak positions with rockets and cannon fire. Other fighters cruised watchfully overhead, on the look-out for prowling Messerschmitts and Focke-Wulfs, but none appeared; in the three days preceding the assault the ten *Luftwaffe* fighter airfields closest to the Wesel area had been pounded by over 2,700 tons of bombs.

But there was still plenty of flak. As the first wave of transports droned over the Rhine at 2,500 feet it began to burst among them, ugly and black. A big four-engined Stirling glider tug was hit and its fuel tanks set ablaze. Its glider slipped its towing cable and veered sharply away as the Stirling reared up vertically before falling over on its back and spinning ponderously towards the ground. The glider pilot managed to land on the bank of the river, yards from a German gun emplacement. An 88-mm round tore through the glider's nose and exploded in the plywood fuselage, killing all inside.

Another glider was hit in mid-air and was hastily cast adrift by its tug. The glider's tail broke off and the rest of the structure spiralled down, shedding fragments and spilling its contents: first a jeep and then soldiers, the luckless men flailing their arms and legs like puppets as they fell to their deaths half a mile below.

Over the Diersfordter Wald, the sky blossomed with thousands of parachutes as the leading waves of transports dropped their cargoes and turned sharply away from the murderous flak.

Over the village of Hamminkeln, American airborne troops of the 513th Parachute Infantry dropped in neat sticks from their c-46 transports. They were in the wrong place. Hamminkeln was strongly defended by German infantry and artillery, and was to have been assaulted by British glider troops equipped with artillery and light tanks.

The Americans took terrible casualties, but organized themselves and went straight into action, launching frontal attacks on dug-in artillery batteries that were all around them. As the vicious skirmishing continued the first Airspeed Horsa gliders of the British 6th Air Landing Brigade swept down to land practically on top of the American infantry. As the gliders skidded to a halt the British airborne troops burst out of them with guns blazing, joined up with the Americans, and stormed Hamminkeln.

While the British and American airborne forces battled to secure their objectives in the face of determined enemy resistance, the spearheads of the British Second Army were forging across the Rhine in their assault craft between the villages of Diersfordt and Mehr. By early afternoon, the airborne brigades had completed the capture of their final objectives, and a strong link-up had been made with the infantry battalions advancing from the river line.

So, in blood and fire and smoke, amid many individual and collective acts of bravery, the Western Allies came to Germany.

In the east the Russian armies were already inside Germany, preparing for the great offensive that would take them across the River Oder to Berlin, forty miles away. In the German capital there was little panic, even though refugees from the east brought daily stories of rape and massacre. Instead, there was a kind of numb acceptance of the inevitable, and here and there a faint gleam of hope that the *Führer's* promise of new and devastating secret weapons would yet bring salvation to the dying *Reich*.

The pinched-faced, hungry-looking people who threaded their way through the rubble of Berlin's Grünewaldstrasse, on their way to join one of the interminable bread queues, took little notice of the army trucks that were parked outside number thirty-five, an imposing building whose windows were now boarded over and whose facade bore the scars of Allied bomb-splinters.

Heavily armed ss troops stood around the trucks, facing outwards. No one stared at them; it was not healthy to stare at the ss. Other soldiers were loading wooden crates into the backs of the trucks. There was nothing strange about that; most government buildings in Berlin had already been evacuated, their personnel and documents moved south to the comparative safety of the Bavarian mountains.

A small group of men stood to one side, surveying the proceedings. They seemed dejected. All wore civilian clothing. Some were quite young, in their middle twenties perhaps, while others were middle aged. This in itself was odd, because most German men in those age groups had long since been conscripted into the army. The men hovered uncertainly around an untidy pile of suitcases.

The last of the wooden crates was brought out, and the heavy door slammed shut on the now-deserted building. One of the civilians, older than the rest, looked up sadly at the name chiselled in Gothic lettering above the door: GERMAN RESEARCH INSTITUTE.

Professor Werner Melzer had spent most of his working life within those walls, engaged, as he had believed, on projects which in the long run would be for the benefit of all mankind. Now it had come to this. His life's work, encapsulated in a few wooden boxes, bearing with it the terrible consequences of his achievement. Since he had discovered how his theories were even now being put to the practical test elsewhere in Germany, Werner Melzer had not slept. He had even contemplated taking his own life.

The senior ss officer came striding up and addressed Melzer, crisply but politely. 'We are ready, Herr Professor. Will you and your colleagues please board the second truck?'

Melzer stared at him, and spoke for all the other scientists. 'What about our families?' he asked. 'What will become of them?'

The ss officer gave a small frown of annoyance. 'I have already explained to you that they will be safe,' he snapped. 'They are being collected at this very moment and will be brought to your new place of work. Now, please get aboard without further delay. Time is short.'

It was useless to protest. Melzer nodded to his colleagues, who picked up their suitcases and made for the designated truck. The younger ones climbed in first, then extended their hands to help up the older men.

As the convoy moved off, it passed a group of boys, aged about fourteen or fifteen, making friends with a stray dog as was the wont of boys everywhere. The difference was that these youths wore uniform and carried guns, and were defenders of Berlin. The ultimate sacrifices, thought Melzer, on the altar of a madman.

And yet — perhaps not the ultimate sacrifices, if the unthinkable came to pass.

*

In New Mexico, on the other side of a war-torn world, it was four thirty in the morning, and another scientist was unable to sleep, his mind buzzing with formulae. They were getting close, he knew that, very close indeed to the culmination of the years of effort, but he would never be certain that they had got everything right until the device was actually built and tested. A quietly restrained air of excitement was sweeping through Los Alamos, and the small group of men who knew precisely what this project was all about were already speaking amongst themselves in tones that were almost reverent about something they knew as Trinity.

It was something so stupendous, so unbelievable, that only their trained scientific minds enabled them to push aside a natural tendency to regard what would soon happen with a mixture of awe and fear. Such feelings were understandable, for if progress continued at the present rate, within four months — perhaps much less than that — they would ignite the fires of the sun on the plains of Alamogordo.

He got quietly out of bed, careful not to disturb his sleeping wife, and made his way towards the kitchen, intent on making himself a cup of coffee and maybe fixing a sandwich. He often got hungry about this time in the morning, and it was over coffee and a sandwich that he did some of his best thinking.

It was fortunate that he was passing by the telephone when it rang. He grabbed the instrument quickly before its insistent shrilling could rouse his wife. It had to be an internal call for there were no outside lines from Los Alamos. Also, he thought, it had to be urgent, for he could not recall having received a telephone call at this time in the morning before.

He was right. The voice on the other end of the line was crisp and charged with tension. 'I'm glad you're awake,' it said. 'Something's happened you ought to know about. Don't go back to sleep. I'll be there in ten minutes.'

General Leslie R. Groves was as good as his word. Ten minutes later, on the dot, his jeep rolled up outside the bungalow and the scientist let him in, noticing as he did so that an armed MP had taken station on the verandah. The general's face was deadly serious, and he did not waste time.

'You'd better sit down, Oppie,' Groves said. 'I have to tell you that the German experiment at Haigerloch has reached criticality.'

Dr J. Robert Oppenheimer, without taking his eyes off the general's face, felt behind him for the arm-rests of a chair and lowered himself slowly into it. He fished absent-mindedly in his pocket for his pipe and tobacco, then remembered that he was wearing a dressing-gown. Suddenly, he felt very cold.

'When?' he asked in a quiet voice.

Groves shook his head slowly. 'That's the problem. We don't know for sure. It may have been as much as a month ago. And if they've managed to cut some corners — ' He left the sentence unfinished. Oppenheimer finished it for him.

'They might have caught up with us, even bypassed us. My God, it doesn't bear thinking about.' He rose abruptly. One of his hands fluttered nervously.

'General, I don't care what time of day it is. I need a drink. How about you?'

Groves nodded. 'Sure. Scotch, if you have any.' Oppenheimer crossed to a drinks cabinet and poured two stiff measures of whisky. He handed one of them to the army officer, who toyed with the glass and stared thoughtfully into the amber liquid.

'Oppie,' he said, 'you're the expert. In your opinion, do they have any chance — any outside chance at all — of building a uranium bomb in the time that's left to them?' Oppenheimer too looked into his glass, as though gazing into a crystal ball in search of inspiration and guidance. It was as though a terrible weight had descended on his shoulders. There was a long silence before he responded. At length, he spoke: 'We know the line of research they've been following, and since our people captured Strasbourg last November we've been assuming that the Germans were at least two years behind us in atomic research.'

He referred to the seizure by American forces, in November 1944, of a mass of documents at Strasbourg University relating to German research into nuclear physics. The documents had been thoroughly examined by the members of an Allied scientific mission code-named Alsos, whose task was to follow the Allied armies into Germany and if possible round up enemy scientists who had been engaged in top-secret military projects. The so-called Uranium Project had headed the list of priorities, and the contents of the Strasbourg papers had brought profound relief to Oppenheimer and his colleagues who were engaged in similar work in the United States.

Oppenheimer now felt that relief rapidly evaporating, to be replaced by a cold dread. 'The Germans know all about the theory behind building a uranium bomb,' he went on slowly. 'They've known it for a long time. They also know the approximate dimensions of such a weapon, and in that respect they were a long way ahead of us. You've seen the evidence.'

Groves nodded, his mind flashing back to an intelligence report that had come out of occupied Czechoslovakia early in 1944. It told of several Heinkel 177 bombers which had been flown into the Letov factory near Prague for special modifications. At least one of the aircraft had been fitted with a massive bomb bay, twenty-four feet long, which — according to a loose-mouthed engineer — was to carry a devastating secret weapon that would win the war for Germany at a single stroke.

There could be only one such weapon.

'It caused a lot of concern at the time,' Groves commented. 'We thought that a German bomb was just around the corner. Then we realized they'd jumped the gun and were nowhere near building one — or so we believed,' he added grimly.

'We had good reason to believe that,' Oppenheimer said. He had no need to elaborate; Groves knew as much, and in some cases more, about the obstacles that had lain in the path of German atomic research as he did himself.

Some of those obstacles had been placed by the Allies themselves. In 1942, for example, gallant Norwegian commandos had sabotaged a factory at Rjukan which had been producing supplies of deuterium for the enemy; deuterium, popularly known as heavy water, was one of the substances which — when used as a jacket, or moderator, around an atomic reactor — sustained the atomic fission process. Oppenheimer's team used graphite for the same purpose.

Not only had the Norwegians sabotaged the factory; they had also sent a ferry that was carrying drums of the stuff on the first leg of its journey to Germany to the bottom of a lake.

The second major obstacle to German success was that they had been slow to set up a factory for treating uranium, in order to produce the necessary uranium-235 isotope. Several kilogrammes of fissile material were needed — a 'critical mass' — for the functioning of an atomic reactor or, for that matter, of a bomb.

It seemed, now, that the Germans had overcome these setbacks. But where was the work being carried out — and, more importantly, had the breakthrough come too late?

It was as though Groves had read Oppenheimer's thoughts.

'It's got to be in the Stuttgart area,' he said thoughtfully. 'Do you remember that hell of a scare we had last November, when air reconnaissance showed a lot of industrial plants being set up almost overnight in a string of valleys near Hechingen?'

Oppenheimer nodded. 'Sure. Frightened the pants off us. We really thought they'd got it together, that it was a carbon copy of our operation here. There were fourteen factories, as I recall, all served by railway spurs and power lines. Then we discovered that they were extracting low-grade oil from shale.'

'Well, I'm beginning to wonder if we just might have been wrong,' Groves said. 'There's no doubt at all that their scientists have managed to achieve criticality — our source on the other side is impeccable.'

Oppenheimer did not bother to ask about the nature of the source. He knew that Groves would give him no answer.

Instead, he said: 'If they've got this far, there's nothing to stop them building a uranium bomb. If only I knew when they went critical, I might have some idea of the time scale, but I don't. As it is, we have to assume a worst case situation. We have to assume that they are in the process of building an operational device right now, and that they may be only weeks away from using it. We need more information, General, and quickly.'

Groves nodded. 'I've considered asking for a full-scale parachute assault on Hechingen, but it's too far from the main battle area. It wouldn't work. Hechingen appears to be heavily defended, mostly by us units. Remember what happened to the British at Arnhem; we don't want to fall into that kind of trap. I think the answer may be to infiltrate with a special forces' team — not just to make a reconnaissance, but to do some damage. I'm getting down to work on that idca right away.'

Groves frowned and set his glass aside, the drink untouched. 'Oppie, there's so much to be done. My head's buzzing with all the possibilities, and most of 'em I don't want to think about, not right now.'

There was nothing more to be said. Oppenheimer accompanied Groves to the door.

On the threshold, the general paused. 'I'm truly sorry to have got you out of bed with this news, Oppie,' he said. 'I realize it's going to put you under a great deal more pressure. I'd be grateful if you'd keep it under your hat, for the time being.'

Oppenheimer shrugged. 'I was up anyway, General. Couldn't sleep, for some reason. A premonition, maybe. And don't worry — I'll keep it to myself.'

After Groves had gone, Oppenheimer made himself a strong coffee and poured the general's untouched whisky into it. Afterwards, he peeped into the bedroom; his wife, Katherine, was still sleeping soundly.

He took a sip of his drink, and was not surprised to find that his hand was trembling slightly. Something kept flashing through his mind, a line from the *Bhagavad Gita*, the sacred epic of the Hindus, uttered by Sri Krishna, the Exalted One, lord of the fate of mortals: 'I am become Death, the shatterer of worlds.'

CHAPTER TWO

Mist drifted in waves across the River Ems, thickened by the smoke that curled from a stricken Sherman tank. The Sherman had almost reached the far end of the only intact bridge over the river before an armour-piercing shell from an 88-mm anti-tank gun had torn into its hull. None of the crew had got out.

The other spearhead tanks of the 4th Canadian Armoured Division had hurriedly slewed off the road leading to the bridge and had taken cover in the ruins of Meppen, most of which lay on the west bank of the river.

It was impossible to locate the position of the lethal enemy eighty-eights which must be dug in somewhere beyond the town. They would massacre anything that tried to move across the bridge. The commander of the leading tank squadron swore. He had no choice but to wait until the mist cleared; then, if he could pinpoint the anti-tank gun positions, he could call in the Typhoons to deal with them. God knew how long it would take. Meantime, the Germans would be building more obstacles in the path of the Canadians' dash towards Oldenburg.

'What the hell?'

The tank commander half-turned in his turret, eyes widening, as three jeeps came roaring down the road. As they swept past, heading for the bridge at top speed, he saw that each one was armed with a Bren light machine-gun.

'Crazy bastards,' the Canadian muttered. 'They'll be killed for sure!'

The three jeeps rumbled on to the bridge without slackening their pace. From somewhere out in front a heavy machine-gun chattered and tracer lanced through the air towards them, the bullets glowing in the grey mist.

Something red and fiery streaked inches above the speeding jeeps, its flat trajectory taking it on to explode among the rubble behind the tanks. It wasn't often, thought the Canadian tank commander abstractedly, that you actually got to see an 88-mm shell. Usually, the first indication you had of one was a hell of a clang, and then your tank stopped. If you were lucky, you got out. Mostly, you didn't.

He suddenly realized that the jeeps, miraculously, were across the bridge. They had bypassed the burning Sherman and were now little more than vague outlines in the fog, spreading out as they headed off towards the left. He wondered how the Germans had managed to spot them — or for that matter the Sherman — while they were still on the bridge. The bastards must have some sort of special sight that could penetrate fog.

Each of the jeeps carried a crew of three. The men ducked instinctively as more tracer came at them, but it went wide.

In the leading jeep, which had now left the road and was bouncing over the uneven surface of a meadow, Major Callum Douglas clung on grimly and made a careful note of the direction from which the enemy fire was coming. He tapped the shoulder of the driver.

'That way, Brian,' he yelled. 'Towards that copse over there! We'll skirt round it and get behind them.'

Douglas knew that the copse was bound to be defended, but it was a risk they would have to take. It would give them the concealment they needed to approach the enemy gun position.

As the distance between the jeep and the copse narrowed, a burst of heavy machine-gun fire came from among the trees, causing the driver, Sergeant Brian Olds, to swerve violently as the bullets sent clods of earth flying from the ground a few feet to one side. In the rear of the vehicle, Corporal Ron Barber, manning the Bren on its special mounting, cuddled the butt of the weapon against his cheek and fired back, seeking out the spot where he thought the enemy MG might be positioned. The gunners in the other two jeeps, speeding along abreast of Douglas's vehicle, had also opened fire, raking the edge of the copse in short bursts.

The jeeps crashed into the undergrowth between the trees and stopped, concealed from the view of the enemy machine-gun position. Douglas and the others jumped out and took cover behind the tree trunks; the gunners unshipped their Brens and threw themselves down in the bracken, clipping fresh magazines in place.

They crept forward among the trees, making short dashes from trunk to trunk. Presently they reached a clearing and froze into motionless shadows at its edge, waiting and watching for signs of movement. They did not have to wait for long. After a couple of minutes half a dozen steel-helmeted Germans came into sight, advancing hesitantly, virtually crouching, in an extended line.

Amateurs, thought Douglas. Poor bloody amateurs. He felt almost sorry for them as he and his men shot them down.

The echoes of the gunfire died away. One of the Germans moved feebly, then was still. For a few moments there was an unreal silence. Then, from the trees on the far side of the clearing, a voice arose, shrill and terrified.

'*Nicht schiessen! Um Gottes willen, nicht schiessen! Wir kommen heraus!*

Douglas beckoned to one of the men who lay close by. 'Liam! Sort this out, will you?'

Captain Liam Conolly, Douglas's second-in-command, was a fluent German speaker. He had lived in Germany for some time before the war, and had left the country on one of the last trains to cross the frontier before the outbreak of hostilities. He had served alongside Douglas for three years, and his linguistic talent had got them out of more than one dangerous situation.

Conolly shouted across to the Germans, ordering them to come out with their hands high. After a few moments' hesitation they emerged from among the trees. Their uniforms seemed baggy, their helmets oversized. There were a dozen of them.

Slowly, as the Germans approached, Douglas stood up. 'Why, they're only bits of bairns!' he exclaimed, lapsing back into his native Scots in his amazement.

'Aye. Bits o' bairns with machine-pistols. Bloody Hitler Youth. We were warned about them, sir.'

The speaker was Sergeant-Major Stan Brough. Like Conolly, he had served with Douglas for the past three years and, in his bluff Yorkshire fashion, had proved to be a tower of strength time after time when the going was rough. Douglas heeded his warning, but noticed that the Germans were not carrying weapons.

'Come over here,' Conolly shouted. 'Walk slowly, and keep your hands up!'

The Germans advanced as they were ordered, and stopped a few yards short of the British soldiers. One of them, obviously the ringleader, stepped out in front of the rest and gave a Nazi salute. Despite his defiance, Douglas saw that he was white faced and shaking with fear. He could not have been more than sixteen years old.

One of his colleagues spoke sharply to him, and what remained of his defiance evaporated. He was close to tears. Douglas tried to read his face. What did the water that brimmed in his eyes signify? Shame, self-pity, degradation perhaps, or the sudden realization that all the promises his master had made were as empty as the future?

Conolly asked him where the machine-gun post was located. The youth looked away and remained tight lipped. It was the other boy who spoke. He had removed his helmet; no one had noticed him lower his hands, but it did not seem to matter. He had fair hair, and a face that would not have been out of place in a cathedral choir.

The boy told Conolly that the MG post was positioned some two hundred metres away. The 88-mm gun itself was dug in behind an embankment beyond the wood, commanding a good field of fire. Both positions, the boy said, were manned by *Waffen* ss troops.

Conolly translated. 'He also says that this joker here' — indicating the youth who had given the Nazi salute — 'wanted to go on fighting to the bitter end, but the others persuaded him otherwise. Apparently he's a fanatical little sod.'

'He doesn't look particularly fanatical now,' Douglas observed. 'Let's see what they've got in their pockets.'

He was hardly surprised when their pockets revealed nothing of interest. A few personal odds and ends — family photographs and the like — and that was all.

'Better get this lot off the premises,' he said. 'Liam, tell them to scarper across to the bridge, and to keep their hands up. Tell them they'll come to no harm if they do as they are told.'

Conolly explained Douglas's orders to the Germans, who at once set off at a run. Douglas watched them pass through the fringe of trees at the edge of the copse and out into the meadow beyond, bunched into a tight little knot as though clinging together for greater safety, their hands held high.

They had gone less than a hundred yards when the Spandau opened up with its characteristic snarl. The little knot of runners disintegrated, the figures sprawling and tumbling like broken puppets as the bullets ripped into them. A terrible screaming rent the air. One of the boys, the one with fair hair who had spoken with Conolly, dragged himself to his feet again and came staggering back towards the copse, his arms stretched out in front of him as though in supplication. He was screaming for his mother.

A burst of fire bowled him over backwards, and he lay still. The figures on the ground jerked as more fire from the Spandau sought them out. After that, nothing moved.

It was incomprehensible, part of the madness of these last terrible days that marked Germany's bloody twilight.

'Bastards!' Conolly said quietly. 'The bloody bastards!'

Douglas's face was white with fury. He had difficulty in keeping his voice steady. 'All right,' he said. 'Let's go and get them!'

Three of his team skirted round the edge of the clearing and took up watchful positions on the other side while the rest paused briefly to examine the bodies of the enemy they had shot earlier. They were mostly middle-aged men and one or two could even be described as elderly; they bore the decorations of a previous war. The thought struck Douglas that a burst of fire over the heads of these men might have been enough to persuade them to surrender, but there was no time to dwell on that now. In any case, they would probably have suffered the same fate as the Hitler Youth boys.

Douglas and his men worked their way into the centre of the copse and approached the enemy MG post from the rear, using all their considerable skill to get in as close as possible before being detected. The post was defended by a ten-man infantry platoon, spaced out in individual foxholes.

The fire-fight, when it came, was brief, savage and one-sided. It was heralded by a shower of accurately placed grenades from the British soldiers. The grenades killed or wounded at least half the defending ss troops and threw the rest into confusion. Some tried to leave their foxholes for more secure positions among the trees; they were shot down as they ran. It was all over in less than forty-five seconds.

The British advanced through drifting tendrils of gun-smoke. Conolly paused to bend over the body of one of the enemy. He peered at the armband on the man's uniform, then straightened up and addressed Douglas.

'29th *Waffen* Grenadier Division,' he announced quietly. 'Russians, fighting on the German side.'

They pushed on through the trees. The mist was beginning to clear, and a pale gleam of morning sunshine filtered through the branches.

When they reached the machine-gun post, they found it abandoned. The Spandau's breech mechanism had been removed, rendering the weapon useless.

'Looks like they've gone to find a better 'ole,' Brough announced.

Douglas nodded. 'Probably decided it was safer with their pals at the eighty-eight,' he said. 'Let's take a look at it.'

They went on cautiously in single file until they reached the southern edge of the copse. Going down on their bellies, they crawled forward until they were able to obtain a good view of the ground beyond. The 88-mm gun was exactly where the unfortunate Hitler Youth had said it would be, dug in behind an embankment that was intersected by the road leading from Meppen. It was mounted on some kind of armoured vehicle which Douglas did not recognize; probably a last-ditch modification, he thought, to give some protection to the gun's crew.

The gun was just over a hundred yards away. He scanned the surrounding area carefully with his binoculars, but could see no sign of any defensive infantry positions. He turned and beckoned to two of his men, Troopers Davies and Carter, who hurried up to lie beside him.

'What do you reckon?' he asked. 'Can you get it with the PIAT?'

The PIAT — Projector Infantry Anti-Tank — was a kind of mortar which had been originally designed for use by airborne troops. It fired a three-pound projectile over a range of a hundred yards or more by means of a coiled spring that was so powerful it needed two men to cock it. The projectile could be fitted with either a round-tipped detonator for soft targets, or a hollow-nosed one for use against armour. It could be fired from the prone position or -with greater difficulty — from the hip. It was not the most accurate of weapons, but it was quite capable of stopping most types of tank. Against a gun emplacement, its effect was lethal. Davies and Carter carried the projector and its mortar bombs slung about their persons.

Davies took a long look at the enemy gun. The top of its armoured hull was just visible above the embankment. The barrel of the gun stuck out like a drainpipe on the other side.

'We'll have a go, sir,' he said presently. 'Give us a hand, Matt.'

Together, they cocked the weapon. Davies lay down in the prone position and Carter fitted a mortar bomb in place.

Davies took careful aim and squeezed the trigger. The spring uncoiled with a thud and a recoil that pushed Davies back several inches. The round shot out over the open ground towards the gun emplacement, wobbling a little as it flew. It embedded itself in the earth of the embankment and failed to explode.

'Bugger it,' Davies muttered, rubbing his shoulder. 'Let's have another go.'

Working quickly, they cocked the PIAT again and Carter inserted a second round. Davies made a slight adjustment to his aim and curled his index finger round the trigger. He squeezed it very gently, releasing his breath as he did so.

Nine pairs of eyes followed the projectile's progress. This time, it missed the top of the embankment by inches. The watching men heard a metallic clunk as it struck the gun-carrier's armoured hull.

A split second later, the whole gun emplacement exploded as the mortar bomb detonated among the gun's stacked ammunition. A great geyser of smoke and flame burst into the air, accompanied by a deafening roar. In the copse, the men burrowed into the moist undergrowth as metal fragments rained down among the trees.

As the echoes of the explosion reverberated across the countryside, Douglas jumped up and asked if anyone was hurt. His voice sounded flat and dead in his own ears. Luckily, no one had suffered injury except Olds, who had collected a small fragment in his forearm. He plucked it out without difficulty, wincing as he did so, for it was red-hot.

'Well done, lads,' Douglas said, addressing Davies and Carter. 'Bull's-eye. Stan, get off a flare. The tank boys can get on the move now. Everybody back to the jeeps. We'll do a recce some way up the road.'

Brough's flare was not really necessary. Even as he fired it from the edge of the copse, he saw the Canadian tanks beginning to cross the bridge in single file. Satisfied, they hurried after the others to where they had left the jeeps.

The vehicles skirted the smoking wreck of the enemy gun. Douglas did not feel inclined to investigate it; there was no possibility that anyone might have survived the terrific blast. The jeeps turned left on to the road and followed it for a mile and a half until they came to a fork. Here, the roadsides were littered with the debris of a retreating army; abandoned trucks and light vehicles, empty boxes and fuel drums. Most of the vehicles were intact, except where pick-axes had been driven through the radiators to render them useless; they must have been abandoned through lack of fuel.

Douglas raised a hand to halt the jeeps and scanned the flat land ahead through his binoculars, examining the few hamlets and isolated farmhouses within his field of view. They seemed deserted, but any one of them could harbour anti-tank guns. There was no sign of any German tanks; if there were any, they were probably concentrated in and around Haselünne, the next place of any importance along the road.

The air drummed with sound. Douglas looked up into a sky that was now virtually clear and saw a squadron of Typhoons, heading into enemy territory. They were flying in pairs, spread out in a long line. He saw that they carried rockets under their wings. He himself had been a tank commander earlier in the war; he decided that he would not like to be one now.

He glanced back. The leading Shermans were trundling up the road, and he ordered the jeeps on to the grass to let them pass. The first tank drew abreast and ground to a stop. Its commander peered down at Douglas from the turret hatch.

'Thanks, you guys,' he shouted, grinning. 'That was quite a display. You commandos, or something?'

'Special Air Service,' Douglas told him. 'We were detailed to scout ahead of you and to keep an eye on your flanks. Looks like the road ahead is clear — the opposition seems to have left in a hurry.' He indicated the abandoned vehicles.

The Canadian nodded. 'Okay. We'll press on. Nice to have you around. See you later; I guess you deserve your breakfast.'

'Well, he's right about that,' Douglas observed as the tanks moved on. 'Let's have a brew-up and something to eat. We'll catch up with them later.'

Olds quickly got a brew of tea going and they delved into their rations, making a frugal meal of bully beef and biscuit. Conolly munched with a thoughtful expression on his face.

'Maybe we should investigate those farms over there, Boss,' he said. 'Should be some eggs, and maybe the odd pig.'

'I doubt it very much,' Douglas told him. 'It's my guess the Huns will have eaten everything that moves by now. Hello — what's this?'

Conolly turned and looked back along the road. A motor cycle was racing down it at considerable speed, its rider skilfully avoiding the tanks that still churned on in a seemingly never-ending stream. He pulled off the road and dismounted stiffly, pushing up his goggles.

Douglas stood up, brushing biscuit crumbs from the front of his battledress. The dispatch rider caught sight of his rank badges and saluted.

'Major Douglas, sir?'

Douglas nodded, returning the salute. 'Yes. What can I do for you?'

The motor cyclist fumbled in the pocket of his leather jacket and handed a buff envelope to the SAS officer. Douglas experienced a familiar sinking feeling in the pit of his stomach.

'It's from Thirty Corps, sir,' the dispatch rider said.

Douglas tore open the envelope and extracted the single sheet of flimsy message paper that was inside. He scanned the typewritten words on it, a puzzled frown creasing his brow, then addressed the motor cyclist: 'All right. Thank you. There is no reply.'

The man saluted again, remounted his machine and went back the way he had come.

Still puzzled, Douglas drew Conolly and Brough to one side. He brandished the message slip. 'I don't understand this,' he said. 'It says we are to report immediately to a Group Captain Sayers at Rheine airfield. The whole of the detachment. That's all. Where the hell is Rheine?' he added as an afterthought.

'It's about thirty miles due south of here,' Conolly said. 'About half way between here and Münster. It was a Hun fighter base before we captured it; they operated those new jets of theirs from it. Don't you remember — that Australian pilot we gave a lift to the other day after he'd baled out mentioned it.'

'So he did,' Douglas said thoughtfully. 'Well, we'd better do as we're told. Let's get packed up and on the road. It all seems a bit odd, though, but I'm not going to argue with the signature on this message.' It was the signature of a very high-ranking officer indeed.

From force of long habit, Douglas took out his lighter and set fire to the sheet of paper. He watched it crumble away to ashes, then climbed into the jeep alongside Olds. The latter whistled cheerfully, even though his forearm was stinging badly where the piece of shrapnel had penetrated it. Douglas asked him what he was so happy about.

'Oh, I was just thinking about getting back to the farm when all this is over,' Olds told him. He had been a farmhand in Norfolk before the war, and seemed just as much at home in the German countryside as in his own native fen country. Olds could smell danger a mile off, just by observing the behaviour of birds.

'It can't be long now,' he added. 'We've been through a lot, haven't we? Funny to think how much has been crammed into the last few years. Still, it'll all be over soon, and we can go home.'

Douglas smiled. It was just about the longest speech he had ever heard Olds make. And it was true: they had been through a lot, and it was nothing short of a miracle that most of them were still around to talk about it. Douglas's team — 's' Detachment of the 1st Special Air Service Regiment — was the most experienced special forces' unit in the British Army, and probably for that matter in any army. They had been in and out of occupied Europe on clandestine operations several times before D-Day, and had pulled off some astounding successes. It would be something to write about one day, thought Douglas, who had always had an inclination to put pen to paper.

The jeeps stopped once to refuel in the town of Lingen and then pushed on as quickly as possible over roads congested with military traffic of all kinds, much of it heading south towards the Ruhr, where isolated pockets of enemy resistance were being mopped up. From time to time, they passed hastily-erected compounds crammed with enemy prisoners. They went through several villages; many of the houses that still stood were festooned with white flags, but there no sign of any of the inhabitants.

They reached Rheine, where bulldozers were still clearing rubble from the streets, and eventually located the airfield. It had been the target of massive Allied bombing attacks during the weeks before its capture, and gangs of German prisoners, supervised and guarded by British troops, were engaged in filling in craters and searching for unexploded bombs.

The airfield was heavily guarded by troops and men of the Royal Air Force Regiment, patrolling the perimeter in armoured cars. Douglas learned that there were persistent rumours that the base — which was in the process of being occupied by three squadrons of RAF Tempest fighters — might become the target for German resistance groups known as Werewolves. After having had their papers subjected to a close scrutiny, Douglas and his men were allowed through and directed to a small building that stood near the wrecked German control tower.

Douglas went inside, leaving the others still in the jeeps, and after making some enquiries found Group Captain Sayers, who turned out to be the acting station commander. He could shed no light on Douglas's orders, other than that he had to telephone a certain number at the Supreme Headquarters Allied Powers in Europe, which was located in Paris, as soon as the SAS party arrived.

'Haven't a clue what it's all about, old boy,' he said apologetically. 'Sounds pretty high-powered stuff, though. Bring your chaps in and have some tea.'

He reached for the telephone, his eyes taking in the decorations on the left breast of the SAS officer's battle-dress. Distinguished Service Order, Military Cross, French Crois de Guerre, Polish Virtuti Militari — this chap has been around, he thought, his curiosity wide awake.

Sayers replaced the receiver, his face puzzled. 'Some American bloke at the other end,' he told Douglas. 'All he would say is that you're to stay put. It's all very mysterious, I must say. Still, make yourselves at home in the meantime. One thing, though — don't go wandering off. There are unexploded bombs and booby-traps all over the place.'

A little over two hours later, a twin-engined c-47 transport aircraft approached Rheine from the south-west. It circled the airfield once, then came down to land, its engines chugging as it taxied in. It carried American markings on its olive-green camouflage. Douglas and the others, who had been eating sandwiches and drinking tea and watching flights of Tempests taking off and landing, took little notice of it. Its engines remained idling as a dapper us Army officer disembarked and made for the building where Sayers had his office. Presently, he re-emerged and approached the group of SAS men. Douglas at once noticed something unusual about him: apart from his captain's insignia, he wore no distinguishing unit badges.

The American singled out Douglas and threw up a crisp salute. When he spoke, it was in the clipped military accent of West Point.

'Major Douglas, sir? I am Captain DeVine. I have orders requesting you and the men of your command to accompany me to Strasbourg. The airplane is waiting.'

He indicated the c-47 — which was known to the RAF as the Dakota — and handed Douglas a piece of paper. Douglas scanned the words on it and raised his eyebrows. The previous message, the one given to him by the dispatch rider, had carried an impressive enough signature; this one was even more impressive. It was signed by General Dwight D. Eisenhower, Supreme Commander, Allied Forces in Europe.

Douglas looked at DeVine. 'Have you any idea what this is all about?' he asked bluntly. The American shook his head.

'None, Major. I am merely acting as a courier. All I know is that the matter in hand is of the gravest importance. May I ask the major to hurry?'

Douglas nodded. 'All right. Give me a minute or two. I'll have to sign over the jeeps to the local army commander, otherwise I'll probably end up getting a bill for 'em from the War Office.' He turned to Conolly. 'The weapons we take with us, except for the PIAT. Get the men on board, please, Liam.'

Ten minutes later, with a hundred questions pounding unanswered through his head, Douglas was seated in the vibrating fuselage of the c-47 as it climbed away into the southern sky. The immediate future remained a complete mystery; but the importance of whatever lay at the end of the transport's flight was underlined by the sudden appearance of half a dozen p-47 Thunderbolt fighters, which appeared out of nowhere and slipped into position on either side of the aircraft. Someone, it seemed, was taking no chances.

CHAPTER THREE

The ancient and beautiful city of Strasbourg is the metropolis of the Alsace Plain. As well as main road and rail communications, natural and artificial waterways also contribute to its strategic importance. The Rhine-Rhone and Marne-Rhine Canals both end at Strasbourg, joining the city by water with southern and northern France.

The liberation of Strasbourg in November 1944 had been of immense psychological value to the Allies and had given a great boost to the prestige of France, for it was the political capital of Alsace, a province annexed by Germany in 1871 and returned to France in 1918, only to be reoccupied by the Germans in 1940. Fittingly, it had been the French 2nd Armoured Division which had spearheaded the Allied assault of 1944, under cover of the artillery of the United States Seventh Army. Fierce fighting had raged around the city in the weeks that followed, but the occupying Franco-American forces had held on to it, and now there was no longer a threat.

Strasbourg, Douglas noted from the back of the us Army Studebaker truck that had brought his detachment from the airfield, seemed to have escaped the terrible damage that had been inflicted on cities farther to the north in the course of the Allied advances during the spring of 1945. The back of the truck was open, and as it passed through the streets French and American soldiers glanced curiously at the handful of strangers, with their red paratroop berets. That was something that still annoyed Douglas; the Special Air Service had been proud of its own sand-coloured beret, with its badge depicting Excalibur, the sword of King Arthur and the motto 'Who Dares Wins'. It had been sacrificed in the interests of uniformity when, after its early campaigns in North Africa, the Regiment had begun commando operations in Europe.

He looked at the faces of his men. The two troopers, Ed Davies and Matt Carter, were newcomers, but so far they had shaped up very well. The two corporals, Barber and Lambert, had been with him longer, and in various actions had shown themselves to be utterly dependable. Conolly, Brough and Olds had been together as part of the detachment for so long that they could practically read each other's minds —

something that could hardly be said of the other member, Sergeant Bill Mitchell.

Mitch and Olds were firm friends, which had always seemed a little odd to Douglas, because it would have been hard to find two people who were more dissimilar in background and appearance. Mitchell was the son of one of Rhodesia's oldest and wealthiest settler families, and no one but he would ever know what had driven him to enlist in the British Army as a private soldier soon after the outbreak of war. Apart, perhaps, from a strong affinity with nature, the only thing Olds and Mitchell seemed to have in common was that they seldom spoke, and then only in monosyllables.

Douglas had an enormous affection for all of them. He found himself worrying about what was to come; even though he had no idea what might lie in store, he had a firm conviction that it was not likely to be pleasant. His men deserved more than to be placed in undue peril at this late hour. Their faces bore deep lines of fatigue; they all badly needed a rest. He supposed that his own face must show the same tell-tale etchings of approaching exhaustion.

Already, there were the nightmares: awful dreams of death and decay, of falling forever through dark tunnels of time and space. And always, there was a figure, receding from him as he tried to catch up with leaden feet; a blurred, indistinct figure, whose face he never saw, but a face that belonged to only one person — his wife, Colette, safe, thank God, in Scotland with his father. He would awaken from those dreams sick and trembling, his jaws aching from the subconscious grinding of his teeth, soaked in sweat and unrefreshed ...

Douglas suddenly realized that Captain DeVine, who was sitting opposite, was looking at him curiously.

'You okay, Major?' the American asked.

Douglas nodded and mustered a smile. 'Yes, fine,' he lied. 'Just a bit tired, that's all. I could do with a bath to liven me up a bit. I suppose we all could.'

DeVine smiled back. 'That's the first thing on the agenda, Major. We know you've had it pretty rough lately. What order do you want it in — bath, sleep and food?' 'Sounds good to me,' Douglas told him. The others nodded in agreement, except for Brough, who had already nodded off, his chin sunk on his chest.

The truck eventually arrived at a building which looked as though it had once been a college, but which had now been turned into a barracks. The French tricolour and the American stars and stripes flew over it, side by side.

us Army orderlies showed the newcomers to their quarters. Douglas, Conolly and Brough had been allocated rooms of their own; the others shared two to a room. Looking round his billet, Douglas noted that everything was spotlessly clean; there was a fresh cake of soap on the washbasin, and a crisp white towel lay on the bed. There were showers just across the corridor; the plumbing was brand new, and Douglas guessed that it had been installed by the Americans soon after the capture of Strasbourg.

Our Allies, he thought enviously, certainly know how to look after their own.

Douglas stripped off his sweaty clothing and spent ten minutes luxuriating under the shower, smothering himself with lather. He dried himself and returned to his room, burrowing down between newly laundered sheets with a blissful sigh. The crazy thought flashed through his mind that the war, with any luck, might end while he slept. Then he knew no more.

He was awakened by a polite cough. He opened his eyes and saw that it was dusk; a lamp on his bedside locker had been switched on. A young soldier in fatigues hovered over him, a glass in his hand.

'Major Douglas, sir. I hope the major had a good sleep. Captain DeVine's compliments, sir. Dinner will be in a half-hour. My name is PFC Johnson, sir, and I am your orderly. I thought the major might care for something to drink.'

Douglas muttered his thanks, reaching out to take the proffered glass as he sat up. He sipped its contents. The drink was orange juice. *Fresh* orange juice, he thought wonderingly. He had tasted nothing like it for years.

'Marvellous, Johnson,' he said. 'Absolutely marvellous.' He drained the glass and handed it back to the orderly, noticing for the first time that the young man was a light-skinned negro. Johnson flashed a set of perfect white teeth at him.

'Thank you, sir. I have had the major's uniform and underwear laundered. It is on the peg beside the door. I hope you find it to your satisfaction, sir.'

'I'm sure I shall, Johnson,' Douglas smiled. 'And thank you for the VIP treatment. Dinner in half an hour, you say? I'd better get up.'

The orderly excused himself and left. Douglas rose and shaved carefully; even a razor had been laid out for him, but he preferred to use the one he had carried in his pack throughout his army career. He put on his clothing, which had a faint aroma of scented soap about it and was still warm from whatever drying process had been used. His uniform had been given immaculate creases, presumably by Johnson, and he could practically see his face in the toecaps of his boots.

He opened the door and went out into the corridor. Johnson was waiting outside, ready to conduct him to the dining-room. Douglas had a question.

'One thing, Johnson — where are my Sten and Smith and Wesson?'

The American looked at him, puzzled. 'Sir?'

'My sub-machine-gun and pistol. I left them on the bedside locker.'

The young man's face cleared. 'I took the liberty of placing them in the orderly room arms-chest, sir, where they would be safe. Things sometimes go missing around here,' he added meaningfully. Douglas knew exactly what he meant.

The dining-room, Douglas discovered in due course, was used by all ranks, although there was a distinct order of segregation, with officers occupying the top tables, senior NCOS next in line, and so on. A bar ran almost the full length of one wall and Douglas saw Conolly propped against it, talking animatedly to DeVine and another American officer. He went across to join them.

'Ah, Major Douglas,' said the inscrutable DeVine. 'Please meet Major McCoy, of the United States Rangers.'

McCoy, who was as tall as Douglas but considerably broader, with a chest like a barrel, stretched out a ham-like fist and pumped Douglas's hand, grinning.

'Joseph B. McCoy,' he rumbled. 'Callum Douglas,' the other said, scrutinizing McCoy closely without trying to be obvious, and failing. McCoy wore a chestful of medal ribbons, and caught Douglas looking at them. He laughed.

'Don't be fooled,' he said, pointing at himself. 'This one's for markmanship, this one's for unarmed combat proficiency, this one's for stepping off the boat in Liverpool. Ain't a genuine one among 'em.'

Douglas was already beginning to like the other man. 'You Americans are astonishing,' he said, laughing, and the words were meant as a compliment. McCoy wagged a finger at him.

'Hey, now, don't you go calling me an American. I'm Irish, just like Liam here.'

Douglas looked perplexed, so McCoy ventured a short explanation. Despite the fact that he had never seen Ireland, McCoy had never considered himself as being anything other than Irish, a loyalty that had been firmly implanted in several generations of McCoys ever since the first contingent had emigrated to the promised land in the wake of the Great Potato Famine.

'Have a drink, Boss,' Conolly said. 'They've got just about everything here.'

'Thanks,' Douglas said. 'A Scotch wouldn't come amiss.' A large one appeared almost immediately, served with a flourish by a barman who looked as though he had learned his trade in the cocktail bar of a high-class hotel. He wore a white waistcoat with gold braid on it, black trousers and a bow tie. It was all very unreal.

'Just by way of explanation,' DeVine said when the barman was out of earshot, 'you and Major McCoy will be working together. More of that later. First, we eat.'

The meal did nothing to reduce Douglas's envy of the American system. Honeydew melon was followed by a T-bone steak that practically covered the plate, accompanied by all the trimmings; after that there was a massive bowl of fresh fruit and ice-cream, followed by cheese, biscuits and coffee. There was no shortage of wine, nor of Cognac to finish off the feast. Douglas's stomach strained against his trousers. He accepted the cigar McCoy offered him and leaned back gratefully in his chair. All of his men had now arrived, and he noticed that they were carefully paired off with us Rangers who were their equivalent in rank. The whole business, he decided, was being well orchestrated, though to what end he had no idea. At this moment in time, surrounded by the aroma of cigar smoke and utterly replete for the first time since his last leave in Scotland — how long ago? — he did not much care.

The shrill ringing of a telephone, fixed to the wall behind the bar, interrupted their conversation. The barman answered it, and presently came over to the table. He spoke quietly to DeVine, who nodded and addressed the others.

'Gentlemen, please follow me. It is time for your briefing.'

He led the officers from the dining-room. Stan Brough threw a questioning glance at Douglas as he went past, but Douglas could only shrug in reply.

They climbed a flight of stairs to the second floor and went along a corridor until they reached a door that was guarded by two white-helmeted American military policemen. Both carried carbines as well as sidearms. They examined everyone's identity documents, then one of them stepped aside and opened the door.

Several men were seated round a highly polished table, its surface littered with files. Most had red covers, indicating the secret nature of their contents.

Douglas recognized one of the men immediately. The recognition was mutual and the man rose, moving round the table to greet Douglas with a handshake. He was a tall man, with dark, wavy hair that was greying a little and receding at the temples. The face beneath was suntanned, which did not surprise Douglas. Brigadier Sutton Masters, a very senior officer in the British Special Operations Executive, was always tanned, no matter what the time of year.

The last time Douglas had met Masters the latter had been wearing civilian clothing. That had been in London, in the spring of 1944, just before Douglas had taken his team into Poland to destroy a German rocket research centre. Masters had been the head of SOE'S Eastern European Section then; Douglas wondered what he was doing here. Whatever it was, it spelt trouble. Masters always did.

Captain DeVine had clearly had dealings with Masters beforehand, and now he introduced Conolly and McCoy to the brigadier. Masters shook hands with both of them, then turned towards the other men who were seated at the table. Their names meant nothing to Douglas, but he took careful note of them as he shook their hands and registered the individual characteristics of each man.

One of them, introduced as Dr Samuel Goudsmit, was a civilian. Judging from his accent, he also appeared to be of Dutch origin. He had a sharply hooked nose and well-groomed hair that was parted in the middle. His high forehead betokened considerable intellect, and Douglas learned later that he was one of the world's leading physicists. He gave Douglas a friendly smile.

The other two men, both us Army officers, were in uniform. The first, Colonel Boris Pash, had close-cropped hair and a thin smile which, in conjunction with exceptionally brilliant eyes that peered at Douglas through rimless glasses, suggested that he would not suffer fools gladly. The other man, Major Robert Furman, gave the impression of being educated and erudite, which also turned out to be correct.

'Very well, gentlemen, please be seated and let us get down to business.' Masters opened the door briefly, ordered the two guards to let no one near the room, then sat down himself and placed his fingertips together under his chin in a gesture Douglas knew of old. When he spoke, it was to address Douglas in the first instance.

'A year ago, Major Douglas, we sat opposite one another in London and I briefed you on your mission to Poland — in which, if I may say so, you and your men achieved highly commendable success. You may recall that, at the time, you were given certain classified information to the effect that research being carried out by the Allies might lead to a new and devastatingly powerful explosive — one so powerful that a single bomb could destroy an entire city. Our fear was that the Germans might be ahead of us in the production of such an explosive, and were possibly preparing to use it in the warheads of their rocket weapons. As we now know, their efforts were in fact aimed at producing a highly lethal nerve gas for use in these weapons. Your action was instrumental in thwarting their aims.'

Douglas glimpsed appreciative nods from around the table and felt slightly embarrassed. Masters had omitted to mention that one of the key men in that operation, a Polish SOE agent, had been in the pay of the Russians, who as a result had captured the German general in charge of the nerve gas project. It had been a considerable coup on their part, and — for Douglas at least — had destroyed any illusion about the degree of co-operation that existed between the Russians and their western allies.

'However,' Masters went on, 'we now know beyond all doubt that the Germans *have* been pursuing top-level research into what I shall call a super explosive, and there are strong indications that they may be very close indeed to perfecting an operational weapon. At this point I shall hand over to Professor Goudsmit, who will explain to you as simply as possible the principles behind such a device.'

Goudsmit nodded. 'Thank you, Brigadier. Well, gentlemen, as Brigadier Masters suggests, I shall keep this as simple as I can. As you may already know, all matter is made up of small indivisible particles known as atoms. Now, the atoms of certain elements arc fissile — that is to say, they can be split by being bombarded by other particles called neutrons. The process was first demonstrated in 1939 by two leading German physicists, Professors Hahn and Strassman. So, how can this be applied to the production of a super weapon?'

He looked at them mildly, as though addressing the question to a group of university students, then answered it himself.

'In theory, all one has to do is to bring together two masses of a suitable fissile material at very high velocity. When the two masses make contact the fission process occurs, and this sets off what we call an uncontrolled chain reaction. It all happens in a millionth of a second, or so we have calculated. The resulting release of energy, we believe, will produce a devastating explosion. Do you have any questions at this point?'

Conolly had been following the professor's words intently, and it was he who put the first question.

'How much of this — this fissile material would be needed to produce a major explosion?' he asked. It was not at all an obvious question, and Goudsmit was pleased. He nodded appreciatively.

'Thank you, Captain. We have calculated that only a few kilos of the material will be sufficient to produce an explosion equivalent to several thousand tons of a high explosive such as TNT.' He leaned back in his chair, watching them carefully to see their reaction to his statement. It was a predictable one.

'Did you says *tons*? McCoy asked, his voice filled with disbelief. Goudsmit nodded. 'Yes, tons. Now you can have some idea of the magnitude, the awesome potential of the weapon we are discussing.'

After that, the questions came thick and fast. Goudsmit explained some of the problems associated with producing a workable example of what he termed an atomic weapon, but in response to other queries he merely shook his head and assumed a guarded expression. He had clearly been carefully briefed on just how far he could go. In the end, sensing that Goudsmit was keen to plunge into greater detail, Masters cleared his throat, making a polite interruption.

'Thank you, Professor. I think that these officers now have some grasp of what is at stake.' He turned to the American officer seated on his right.

'Colonel Pash, would you be kind enough to take up the briefing?' Pash removed his glasses and placed them carefully on the table in front of him, toying with them from time to time as he spoke.

'First of all,' he said. 'I must explain that I am head of a special group known as the Alsos Mission. If the name puzzles you, it is taken from the Greek language and means 'grove'. The purpose of the Alsos Mission, which has been operating in Europe since shortly after the Allied landings, is to round up German scientists — in particular those engaged in atomic physics research — and to seize as many of their documents as possible. Some of their papers have already come into our possession — in fact they were found right here, in Strasbourg — and lend weight to our fear that the Germans are much more advanced along the road to producing an operational atomic weapon than we previously believed.'

He replaced his spectacles and picked up three folders, handing one each to Douglas, McCoy and Conolly. Douglas noticed that he did not pass one to DeVine, and decided that there must be more to the silent American captain than met the eye.

He opened the folder. It contained a number of photographs, most of them taken from the air. Colonel Pash explained what they depicted.

'As you can see, the first few photographs show a series of factories which the Germans have set up near Hechingen, to the south of Stuttgart. The place is in a long valley, or rather a series of valleys, between two lots of wooded high ground. We've known about it since last November.'

Pash frowned. 'At first, our scientific people were convinced that this was nothing more than a simple, if rather efficient, method of extracting oil from shale. There's a lot of it in the area, as we confirmed when we examined some pre-war German geological records in the Geological

Museum in London. We decided to bomb the factories anyway, but to wait until their construction was somewhat more advanced. As a result, we may have wasted valuable time.'

The American paused, as though gathering his thoughts. 'Since then,' he went on, 'several things have happened that have led us to revise our opinion. The first was the arrival in London, from a secret source in Sweden, of information indicating that the oil shales in the Hechingen region bear uranium, which is one of the fissile elements referred to by Professor Goudsmit. The second was the erection of a great many electricity pylons in the vicinity of the factories — far more than would be needed in the simple extraction of low-grade oil from shale. You see, gentlemen, the production of a uranium bomb requires a great deal of electricity.'

Pash did not elaborate on this last piece of information. Instead, he asked them to examine some more of the photographs. They showed what appeared to be antiaircraft sites, artillery emplacements and armoured fighting vehicles, the latter partly concealed in forest clearings.

'We then learned that a large number of troops, subsequently identified as ss, had moved into the area, together with a lot of equipment, and had set up strong defences in the vicinity of the factories. We asked ourselves why the Germans would wish to defend a minor oil production plant to such a degree, and failed to arrive at a satisfactory answer. Finally, a concentration camp containing several thousand slave labourers has been built nearby. As fast as we bomb the installations — and we have done so on several occasions — they repair the damage. As a matter of fact the bombing has not been particularly effective, because the factories and their ancillary installations are well camouflaged. The heavy flak has inflicted considerable losses on our aircraft, too.'

Pash looked gravely from face to face.

'Gentlemen, a few moments ago Professor Goudsmit mentioned that a uranium bomb would have an explosive force equivalent to several thousand tons of TNT. There is more to it than that — much more. Apart from the blast effect, our scientists have calculated that the release of energy at the moment of explosion would produce temperatures quite literally similar to those in the heart of the sun. Great firestorms would be created, extending possibly miles from the centre of the explosion. There might be other side effects too, about which we know very little as yet.'

'One point we ought to make, Colonel, is that we don't really know whether a uranium device will work at all,' Goudsmit interrupted in a mild tone. 'The theories have yet to be put to a practical test.'

Pash shot a warning glance at him. Goudsmit nodded and fell silent.

'We have to assume that a uranium bomb *will* work,' Pash said firmly, 'and that the enemy may be in a position to use it first. Our task, quite simply, is to stop them.' 'More specifically, Major Douglas, it's going to be up to you to stop them. You and Major McCoy,' Masters said. 'That's why you've been brought here. Douglas, your team is the most experienced of any in this kind of operation. You will have two days to train with Major McCoy and his men and teach them some of your techniques. We can allow you no more time. I should add that the order that this is to be a joint Anglo-American operation comes from the very highest level. You'll have two days to train, one day to make your final preparations, and then you will be infiltrated. Do you have any questions?'

Douglas had a great many, but he decided to save most of them until later. One would do for the moment.

'One thing has been puzzling me, sir. Professor Goudsmit said that this what d'you call it, this uranium device weighs only a few kilos. Does that mean an operational bomb can be dropped by a fighter-bomber, or maybe fired from a long-range howitzer?'

Goudsmit shook his head. 'No, Major. The uranium, fissile element of the device may fit into a relatively compact space, but the explosion has to be triggered by a large amount of high explosive. We have calculated that the total weight of an operational bomb — including the fissile element, explosive and bomb case — will be in the order of five or six tons.'

'But the Germans don't have an aircraft capable of lifting that kind of weight,' Conolly objected.

Colonel Pash looked at him. 'You're wrong, Captain. They do. Take a look at the last photograph in your folder.'

Conolly did so. The picture showed several views of a massive six-engined aircraft and bore the caption 'Junkers Ju 390'. He looked questioningly at Pash.

'The Germans only have two of them,' Pash elaborated. 'They were photographed at the Letov Aircraft Factory near Prague, Czechoslovakia, early last year having modifications made to their bomb bays. According to a very reliable intelligence source, the bays were being lengthened to twenty-four feet in order to carry some kind of super weapon. The dimensions fit in nicely with the space that would be needed to carry a six-ton bomb. Yet another piece fitting neatly into the jigsaw, gentlemen.'

Pash removed his glasses again and polished the lenses carefully with a pocket handkerchief.

'Since they were located at Prague,' he said slowly, 'the two Junkers have cropped up at various other locations. They were last seen some three weeks ago by our reconnaissance aircraft at Rechlin, the German test centre near Berlin.'

'And since then?' Douglas asked.

'And since then, Major, they appear to have vanished from the face of the earth.'

CHAPTER FOUR

The great aircraft seemed to hang motionless in the night sky, three miles above the Atlantic Ocean. The thunderous roar of its six BMW radial engines had long since become a kind of dull, heavy silence, unnoticed by the eight-man crew.

The aircraft, a Junkers 390, was the largest bomber ever built. Its huge wings spanned one hundred and sixty-five feet from tip to tip, twenty feet longer than those of the American B-29 Superfortresses that were steadily pounding Japan to rubble. It was one of only two in existence. Only two, where there might have been hundreds, if the right decisions had been made at the right time.

With bombers such as these, Germany might have shattered London and Moscow, just as the Lancasters and Halifaxes of the RAF and the Flying Fortresses and Liberators of the USAAF — bombers that were almost puny by comparison — had systematically destroyed the great cities of Germany.

Now, in April 1945, it was too late, a fact that caused Hermann Kreipe to wonder for the hundredth time why he had been ordered to fly this mission. No one had given him a reason, except to tell him that he had been picked because he had more experience in flying long-range missions than any other pilot in Germany. So, for that matter, had the rest of his crew.

In the years before the war, all of them had served with Lufthansa, the German airline, and had helped to pioneer several long-range routes to the Americas and the Far East. When the war had brought Lufthansa's long-range activities to a standstill they had been impressed into service with the *Luftwaffe*, which had need of their expertise.

In the spring of 1944 Kreipe and his crew, flying a Junkers 290 transport — the machine from which the Junkers 390 bomber had been developed — had made several non-stop flights from Odessa to Japanese-occupied Manchuria, carrying aero-engines and other special cargoes on the outbound trip and returning with desperately needed raw materials such as rare metals and crude rubber. Those flights, too, had ceased when the Red Army's spectacular advances in the following summer overran the Russian airfields which the Germans had been using.

Kreipe had enjoyed those journeys, which had taken his aircraft almost exactly along Parallel of Latitude forty degrees North, skirting the southern frontiers of the Soviet Union before crossing China's Sinkiang Province and the trackless wastes of the Gobi Desert. They had taken him back to the pioneer flights before the war, times of good food and drink, of spectacular sunrises and sunsets, of limitless vistas stretching away beyond the aircraft's wing-tips. There had been peril too, in towering thunderclouds and raging storms of sand, but that too had all been part of the pattern of his life.

Now it was all gone, just as the future of the Third Reich was now no more than a madman's dream.

The last gamble had failed. The Germans had called the operational plan Autumn Mist, and it had looked fine on paper. In the weeks before Christmas 1944, two Panzer armies, taking advantage of fog and snowfalls that had kept the Allied reconnaissance aircraft on the ground, had secretly moved into position in the Eifel Mountains of western Germany, ready to advance through the Ardennes forests and across the River Meuse, taking the American forces by surprise and forging on to reach Antwerp, a hundred miles away.

Antwerp had just been reopened by the Allies, and massive tonnages of supplies were pouring through it, building up the resources of their armies in readiness for the final offensive into the Reich.

The plan had been formulated on classic *Blitzkrieg* lines. After a tremendous opening barrage, picked assault troops were to have breached the American line in a dozen places, tearing great gaps through which the armour and infantry columns would pour. These would race through the difficult Ardennes terrain without regard for protecting their flanks and capture the vital bridges across the Meuse before the Allies could regain their composure.

Once across the Meuse the second phase of the offensive, a double-pronged drive north-west to Antwerp, was to have begun. The two tank armies spearheading the offensive would be joined by another from Holland, and when Antwerp and the Scheldt Estuary had been taken the Allied forces in Europe would be cut in two and their four armies in the north, the us 1st, us 9th, British 2nd and Canadian 1st could be destroyed. Then, Adolf Hitler had believed, the Allies would be forced to make a separate peace and Germany could switch all her forces to the east, against the Russians.

It was the last desperate gamble of a man in charge of a crumbling Reich, but there were many who had believed it might just succeed. Field Marshal von Rundstedt, the forthright old warrior who was in command of the German forces in the west, was not one of them. His comment on the plan had quickly become legendary among Hitler's top generals.

'Antwerp? If we reach the Meuse we should go down on our knees and thank God!'

The offensive had begun at dawn on the sixteenth of December 1944. Ten days later it lay in ruins, thwarted by unexpectedly dogged American pockets of resistance, especially at a place called Bastogne, and by the swift intervention of Field Marshal Montgomery's British forces in the north.

Then, with the clearing of the skies, all Allied fighter-bombers had come, swarms of them, dealing out destruction on a massive scale to the German armoured columns. Early on New Year's Day, in a desperate bid to bring some respite to the battered ground forces, the *Luftwaffe* had hurled a thousand of its own fighter-bombers against the Allied airfields in Belgium and Holland. They had destroyed over three hundred Allied aircraft, but had lost nearly two hundred of their own.

The Allies could replace their aircraft. The Germans, their industry shattered by incessant bombing, could not. For the *Luftwaffe*, January 1945 had marked the beginning of the end. And now the Allied armies were deep inside Germany.

And now, thought Kreipe, here we are, lumbering over the Atlantic on a seemingly pointless mission. What was more, with two civilians on board. At least, they were wearing civilian clothes under the heavy, heated flying suits they had been given, but to Kreipe's way of thinking they had ss stamped all over them. He knew that they were armed, because he had caught a glimpse of one of them adjusting a shoulder holster to a more comfortable position when he donned his flying clothing.

That made Kreipe rather nervous, even though one of the mysterious men had long since ceased to take an interest in the flight. He was lying on a rest bunk in the main cabin, suffering the miseries of airsickness.

His companion, on the other hand, appeared to be very much on the alert. He appeared to understand fully the principles of air navigation, and had struck up a sporadic conversation with the navigator, peering over the latter's shoulder from time to time to inspect the plotting chart.

It was the sudden voice of the navigator that now interrupted Kreipe's reverie. 'Estimating landfall in thirty minutes, Captain. We are on track.'

'Very well. I had better take over now, Gerhard.'

The co-pilot, who had been flying the big aircraft for the last couple of hours so that Kreipe could take a break, now relinquished the controls and thankfully flexed his tired arms.

'Crew to action stations,' Kreipe ordered. 'And gunners, keep a good look-out. I hope we won't meet with any opposition, but you never know.' The Junkers flew steadily on. The night was clear and frosty, and there was a glow on the far horizon. It grew brighter with every passing second.

'Just look at that,' the co-pilot said in wonder. 'Lit up like a Christmas tree.'

Kreipe made no comment. He had not seen a coastline spangled with the lights of cities for more than five years — if one excluded the light of Germany's cities burning, he thought bitterly.

The navigator, following his instructions, began calling out the decreasing distance between the aircraft and the brightly lit coast. With twenty kilometres still to run, Kreipe swung the Junkers round in a broad turn. He had strict orders not to approach beyond the twenty-kilometre point.

With the distant lights behind it now, the Junkers headed back the way it had come over the dark Atlantic waters. Ahead of it lay a flight of four thousand miles, a thirteen-hour journey along the great circle route that would take it to the south of Greenland and then through the gap between Iceland and the Faeroe Isles before regaining its base at Trondheim, in Norway.

With a sudden shock, Kreipe realized that by the time the Junkers landed, it would have flown further, and remained in the air longer, than any other aircraft in history.

'We can do it,' the man in civilian clothing said. 'Now, at last, we know that we can do it!' He spoke quietly, as though unaware that everyone could hear him over the intercom.

Do what? Kreipe wondered, and felt too tired to care. The relief crew, who had been getting some sleep during the outward flight, could take over now. He would have them wake him as the bomber approached Iceland.

As the Junkers droned on, the weary gunner in the upper turret position, perched on top of the fuselage and facing rearwards, was the last to see the lights of New York as they faded beyond the horizon.

Major Helmut Winter had never seen a Junkers 390. For that matter he had seen very few German aircraft of any type during the long retreat from the east. He had seen plenty of Russian ones, though, during the series of desperate rearguard actions he and his men had fought against the Red Army in Czechoslovakia during the past few weeks — mainly Stormovik assault aircraft, screaming down in waves to pulverize the German convoys with cannon, bombs and rockets. In the spring of 1945, the Red Air Force was mistress of the eastern skies.

Winter looked around him with appreciative eyes, taking in the wooded hillsides that rose around him. The last time he had passed through Württemberg, the province that nestled in the south-western corner of Germany, bounded to the west by the Black Forest and to the south by the Swiss frontier, had been almost exactly five years ago, in April 1940.

Then, as now, the superb forests of oak and beech and fir had been alive with birdsong. All round, the wild raspberries had been pushing up their shoots, and the broom bursting with yellow flowers.

Winter and his men had trained in these hills in readiness for the part they were to play in the events of May 1940 — that hot, heady, never-to-be-forgotten month when the Panzer divisions had crept along the winding roads of the Ardennes and then hurled themselves across the River Meuse in the wake of screaming Stuka attacks to shatter the French Army and come close to ensnaring the British Expeditionary Force at Dunkirk.

Winter had been at the forefront of that romp across France, with the elite fighting troops of the Brandenburg Division — the unit whose task it was to carry out missions of extreme danger, missions that no other unit would touch, often operating deep behind enemy lines. Admiral Canaris, the head of German Military Intelligence, had been its master and it was answerable only to him and the *Führer*, although Winter had

41

always suspected that Hitler was kept in ignorance of many of its activities.

Winter had been a Brandenburger right from the beginning, since October 1939, when the German Company for Special Missions had first been formed at Brandenburg-on-the-Havel. Its recruits in those days had come from the Sudeten SA, from the Free Corps and the Prussian Young Alliance, of which Winter had been a member.

By the beginning of 1940 the unit had reached battalion strength, and on a big, wooded estate near Brandenburg the young volunteers had learned the tricks of their trade. They had learned how to parachute and how to make explosive devices; they had learned to survive for lengthy periods in hostile territory, living off the land. Each man had become fluent in one or more foreign languages.

Their unofficial motto was *Siegen oder Sterben* — Win or Die. In more than five years of war they had done both, on every front.

Helmut Winter had risen through the ranks. As a corporal, with a group of other Brandenburgers, he had entered Norway three days before the German invasion of 9 April 1940, crossing the border from neutral Sweden. When the attack came, he and his comrades had destroyed vital communications links between Oslo and key military installations. A month later, already a sergeant, he had been part of a team that had been dropped into Belgium by Fieseler Storch light aircraft. Wearing Belgian uniforms, the Germans had seized crossing points on the River Meuse and held them until the arrival of the armoured spearheads of General von Bock's Army Group B.

Winter had been commissioned in the field for an action south of the river Somme in June 1940 that had resulted in the capture of a French general and his entire staff. Yet in one sense the mission had been a failure: its real aim had been to kill or capture the troublesome and spirited commander of the French 4th Armoured Division, one of the few Frenchmen determined to fight to the bitter end. But Charles de Gaulle had eluded his would-be killers and had found sanctuary in England.

In August 1940, with the Germans masters of most of western Europe, the Brandenburg battalion had been expanded to the status of a regiment; and in June 1941 it was further expanded to divisional strength in time to take part in Operation Barbarossa — the German invasion of Russia -and the drive eastwards towards the rich oilfields of the Caucasus. The drive had ended at Stalingrad.

Winter had escaped that nightmare, his company having been flown from Russia to North Africa for operations against the British Special Air Service, whose surprise attacks out of the deep desert on German airfields in Tunisia had been a constant thorn in the side of Field Marshal Erwin Rommel, the commander of the Afrika Korps. But when Winter arrived the German cause in North Africa was already lost, the German forces crushed between the British Eighth Army advancing from the Libyan Desert and the American drive from Algeria.

It had seemed to Winter that it had been the defeat in North Africa, rather than the annihilation of the Sixth Army at Stalingrad, that had signalled the start of Germany's progressive collapse. Even the special missions carried out by the Brandenburgers since then seemed to have gone badly wrong, starting with an abortive attempt to kill Tito, the leader of the Yugoslav partisans, in the summer of 1943. That had been followed by more months of murderous fighting on the Russian front, and the literal decimation of the Brandenburg Division.

Winter had gone into Russia on this second occasion with a hundred men. He had brought thirty of them out. Yet the terror he had experienced in Russia was nothing against the horror of being entombed underground for three days in the spring of 1944, when Polish Resistance fighters — assisted, Winter knew, by British commandos — had attacked and blown up the rocket test site on the Baltic coast which he and his men had been defending. The survivors of the attack had been on the verge of taking their own lives, rather than suffer slow starvation, when rescue finally arrived.

He still had nightmares about that experience, sometimes waking screaming in the night. Wild horses, he knew, would be needed to drag him underground again.

He shuddered and a chill ran through him. He glanced sideways at his companion and second-in-command, Captain Franz Warsitz, and wondered if that terrible experience had affected him, too; if so, the captain showed no outward sign.

Both officers were seated in the rear of a *Kubelwagen*, a sturdy light utility vehicle that was roughly the equivalent of America's famous jeep. Its correct designation was Volkswagen Type 82, and thousands were in

43

service throughout the German armed forces. It was one of the few motor vehicles which had proved to be completely at home in the often appalling conditions of the Russian front; its very light weight — just half a ton — prevented it bogging down and it could be manhandled by two men. The vehicle was driven by a young corporal who looked — and probably was — barely seventeen. The *Wehrmacht* was scraping the barrel for manpower, these days.

The *Kubelwagen* was followed by an Opel truck containing twenty soldiers, all that remained of Winter's command. He had no idea why they had suddenly been ordered back into Germany, and he didn't care. In his tunic pocket he carried precise orders telling him where to go, and the knowledge was of great satisfaction to him. Every mile he and his men travelled westwards was a mile closer to the advancing Americans, and Winter had long since made up his mind that it would be infinitely preferable to be taken prisoner by them than by the Russians. He knew that Germany was finished. Nothing could save the Reich now. It could only be a matter of weeks before the end came. There was nothing left now for the Branden-burgers to fight for, but they would go on fighting just the same, if they had to. That was their tradition.

Tradition was all they had left, because the Brandenburg Division existed now in name only. Its former commander, Admiral Canaris, had been implicated in the plot to assassinate Adolf Hitler in July 1944 and was now, or so rumour had it, languishing in a concentration camp under sentence of death. He was only one of five thousand who had fallen victim to Hitler's murderous purge that had followed the July bomb plot. After that the Brandenburg Division had been split up, its personnel assigned for special duties to other units.

Warsitz took out a silver cigarette case and offered its contents to Winter, who took one and gave his second-in-command a light in return. Warsitz inhaled deeply and grimaced.

'God, what I'd give for a decent smoke!' he exclaimed. 'The stuff they put into these things is worse than the shit we used to take from the Ivans.'

Winter grunted in reply but said nothing. He did not voice his thoughts, which revolved around the possibility that they would probably soon be smoking far better quality cigarettes, generously provided by their American captors.

In front of them, the driver sniffed the acrid smoke enviously and thought: miserable bastards, they didn't offer me a cigarette. Maybe they think I'm too young to smoke.

The two vehicles had made steady if slow progress since leaving Ulm some hours earlier, following tortuous roads through the wooded hills and stopping occasionally in some picturesque village — untouched so far by the war — to allow the men to stretch their legs. On one such occasion they had watched with upturned faces as a huge formation of American bombers had passed miles overhead, dragging their vapour trails behind them, the air vibrating with the remote thunder of their engines. They had sailed on like a great shoal of silvery fish, unmolested by flak or fighters, bound for some luckless and unknown target.

Dann Finis Germaniae, Winter had thought philosophically. So this is the end of Germany, written in chalk-marks across the April sky.

Warsitz had been map-reading, passing instructions to the driver from time to time. Now he remarked to Winter that they must be getting somewhere near their destination, denoted by a map reference. The reference in itself was puzzling, because it fixed a position in the middle of a wood. The map gave no indication that there was anything there.

They came upon the road-block quite unexpectedly as they rounded a hairpin bend in the road. It was a formidable obstacle in the form of a Tiger tank. The road was narrow at this point and the armoured giant straddled it completely. Its 88-mm gun pointed menacingly at the approaching vehicles.

'Keep going,' Winter told the driver. 'It's on our side. At least I hope it is,' he added with wry humour.

Several military policemen emerged from the trees by the side of the road and stood with legs astride, submachine-guns at the ready. One of them held up his hand in a signal to stop. The thought crossed Winter's mind that, with the Tiger blocking the road, the gesture was rather superfluous.

The MP relieved the three occupants of the *Kubelwagen* of their identity papers and subjected them to a thorough scrutiny. Others descended on the Opel truck and ordered the soldiers to dismount while their papers were examined too. They seemed to take an unduly long time over the process, but Winter said nothing. He had long since ceased to argue with 'head-hunters'. It wasn't worth it. Maybe, with a company of Brandenburgers at his back, but not now.

At last the MP handed back the papers and gave Winter a grudging salute. 'Proceed half a kilometre along the road, Herr Major,' he said, 'and you will find a track leading off to the right, into the woods. After several hundred metres you will reach another checkpoint, where you will receive further instructions.'

He turned and signalled to a soldier whose head and shoulders were visible above the turret hatch of the tank. A few moments later the Tiger's Maybach engine burst into life, sending a cloud of diesel fumes into the air. The monster reversed off the road in a clatter of tracks, allowing the vehicles to move on.

The young corporal found the track mentioned by the MP and turned on to it, followed by the Opel. As they drove on Winter saw that this was only one of several tracks, forming a criss-cross of roads among the trees. Beside the tracks expertly camouflaged tanks were parked, nestling in the undergrowth like brooding prehistoric monsters. Most were Panthers, with a sprinkling of the formidable Tiger ns. Warsitz looked at his superior officer in surprise.

'I didn't know we had that many left,' he commented.

'Neither did I, Franz,' the other replied. 'And I'd like to know what the hell they're doing here, instead of supporting our front-line troops.'

As the MP had predicted, the two vehicles were stopped a second time, at a point where several tracks converged in a clearing. Once again, the identity papers of their occupants were examined. Winter noted that on this occasion, the checkpoint was manned by soldiers who wore the uniform of the *Waffen* ss. They treated Winter with a good deal more courtesy than the MP had shown.

'Please park your vehicles beside the track, Major,' one of the soldiers said. 'Your men can get something to eat at a field kitchen not far away. We will show them where it is. You and the captain are to report to that trailer, over there among the trees.'

He pointed, and Winter made out a long trailer, its camouflage paint making it practically invisible in the dappled woodland shadows. Radio aerials protruded from its roof, indicating that it was some sort of command post. The door, with steps leading up to it, was guarded by two heavily armed soldiers, also with the twin lightning flashes of the ss emblazoned on their helmets. Yet again, with typical Teutonic thoroughness, the officers' papers were subjected to a minute scrutiny. At length, one of the ss men mounted the steps, knocked on the door of the trailer and went inside. A few moments later he returned, indicating that Winter and Warsitz were to enter.

The door led directly into a large compartment. Maps were taped to the walls, and more were spread out on a table that took up most of the floor space. Sandwiched into one corner, an ss telegraphist wearing headphones sat in front of a radio set.

A man wearing the uniform of an ss *Sturmbannführer*, roughly the equivalent of a colonel in the German Army, was leaning over the table, making pencil marks on one of the maps. He straightened up as Warsitz closed the trailer door and turned to face the newcomers.

He was a tall man, well over six feet, with a round face topped by close-cropped hair. An old duelling scar meandered from his left ear, across his cheek and down past his mouth to the cleft in his chin. He had a very thin moustache. His eyes were grey and piercing, the eyes of a professional soldier and a commander who would tolerate no stupidity.

He smiled, a little unexpectedly, and extended a hand. 'So, Winter, you managed to arrive. I was afraid you might have fallen victim to the *Jabos.*' He referred to the *Jagdbomber*, the Allied fighter-bombers that now roved all over Germany, seeking targets of opportunity.

'And this must be Captain Warsitz?'

Winter stepped aside as Warsitz took the ss officer's hand and smiled inwardly to see a flicker of admiration in his subordinate's eyes as recognition dawned.

He could understand it. Although personally he did not like Otto Skorzeny-the man was a dyed-in-the-wool Nazi -there was no denying that he possessed enormous military flair, and his exploits as leader of Germany's special combat forces had made him a legend in his own time. It was Skorzeny who, in September 1943, had led a formation of troop-carrying gliders to a tiny plateau on the Gran Sasso, where the Italian dictator Benito Mussolini was being held under arrest in an hotel after Italy had switched to the Allied side; in an operation lasting just four minutes, Skorzeny's men had seized the hotel and rescued Mussolini, who was flown in a Storch to Practica di Mare and from there to Hitler's headquarters.

From that time on, there had been no holding the flamboyant ss officer. He had been authorized to form anti-partisan groups — *Jagdverbände* — which were hated and feared throughout occupied Europe. He had ensured the loyalty of the Hungarian Government to Hitler by the simple expedient of arresting its ministers and holding them under threat of death. He had led an armoured brigade in the abortive Ardennes offensive, and groups of his men, wearing American uniforms, had spread confusion behind the enemy lines.

It was not for nothing that *Sturmbannführer* Otto Skorzeny had been called the most dangerous man in Europe.

'Well, Winter,' Skorzeny said, 'I expect you have no idea why you were summoned here?'

Winter shook his head. 'No, sir. None at all. I was just given a map reference ... Apart from that, nothing. No headquarters designation, no idea about anything else. Forgive me, sir, but just what is this all about?'

'All in good time, Winter. First of all, take a look at the map here.'

Winter and Warsitz bent over the table, one on either side on Skorzeny. The latter tapped the map with his crayon.

'I don't have to tell you that the Reich faces a very serious military situation,' he said. Winter and Warsitz exchanged glances over his bent back, each thinking the same thing; that his remark must surely qualify for the understatement of the century.

'In the north,' Skorzeny said, 'our forces in the Ruhr are surrounded. Soon, the Anglo-Americans in the west and the Russians in the east will be racing to capture Berlin. It is my guess that the Russians will be there first.'

He straightened up and faced Winter.

'Here, in the south, the Americans are engaging our forces in the Black Forest. Soon they will seek to penetrate the mountain redoubt of Bavaria, the Reich's final bastion, and join hands with their Russian friends advancing from Czechoslovakia. Then the Reich will be finished. Or so they think.'

Winter looked at him questioningly, and Skorzeny gave one of his thin smiles.

'What would you say, Winter, if I were to tell you that we are in a position to reverse this situation literally overnight? That we can still win the war, even at this late hour, and have our enemies begging for mercy?'

Winter stared the ss officer straight in the eyes for several long moments before speaking.

'With all due respect, sir, I would say that you were deranged.'

This time, Skorzeny laughed out loud and clapped Winter on the shoulder.

'Exactly what I would have said, Major! But before this day is out, I think that you may well have changed your mind. I have much to show you, but first we must eat.'

He picked up one of the telephones that stood in a row on the opposite side of the table, and Winter heard him ordering lunch. After a moment or two, he addressed both officers, his face serious.

'I have brought you here because I have a very special task for you. It is a task I am not prepared to entrust to my ss troops. Once, I would have done so without question, but nowadays the ss spirit — and perhaps loyalty — has been thinned by too much foreign blood. I need Germans, good Germans, for what I have in mind. Besides, the combat record of the Brandenburg Division is superb, and in some respects unique.'

He noticed Winter's mystified look, and laughed again.

'Don't worry, Winter. Soon you will know everything, including how it feels to be a member of a privileged group of people whose destiny it is to change the course of history!'

CHAPTER FIVE

The sun was up, but an early April morning frost still glittered on the tree branches. The nine men left visible puffs of breath behind them as they advanced cautiously through the wood, one careful step at a time, alert for signs of danger.

A twig cracked under someone's foot and the whole platoon froze. Major Jim McCoy, in the lead, swivelled his body and looked back along the line of men in annoyance. The culprit was a young soldier who was fourth in line. His face reddened under his steel helmet and he shrugged apologetically. McCoy glared at him for a few moments, then waved the men forward.

They had gone less than a hundred yards when all hell broke loose. Explosive devices that sounded like grenades erupted amongst them and an ear-splitting rattle of gunfire burst through the trees. The men didn't wait for McCoy's yell of 'Hit the dirt!' They were already there, burrowing into the undergrowth in a desperate bid to find whatever cover was available. Bullets crackled over their heads, sending splinters of wood leaping from the tree trunks.

The soldier who had been last in line had flung himself under a bush. He lay there panting, his eyes flicking from side to side. Long moments passed as the echoes of the gunfire died away.

An iron-hard hand clasped itself over his mouth and nostrils, cutting off his breath. Something sharp pricked the side of his throat. He began to struggle in panic.

A voice whispered softly in his ear. 'No use struggling, son. I'm afraid you're dead. Now, I'm going to relax my hold. Not a peep out of you, mind, there's a good lad.'

The vice-like grip relaxed and the soldier drew in a shuddering gulp of air. His eyes swivelled sideways again, to the extent of his peripheral vision.

Liam Conolly gave him a broad grin and winked at him.

After a few more moments, Douglas's voice sounded through the trees. 'All right, you can get up now. Come on out.'

McCoy and the others did as they were told. McCoy faced a smiling Douglas and threw his helmet on the ground in anger that was not altogether feigncd.

'God damn it, Major!' he roared. 'You didn't say you'd be using live ammunition!'

'What do you think the other side uses?' Douglas asked mildly. 'Balloons on sticks?'

McCoy grunted and gave a discomforted scowl. Douglas decided that a little reassurance was in order.

'Don't worry, Jim. You've all done pretty well. Much better than yesterday. You got this far, which is a big improvement.'

'But damn it,' McCoy objected, 'we're Rangers! With all the training we've had —'

'Training is no substitute for action, Jim,' Douglas interrupted. 'We've all seen plenty of that, but your turn has yet to come. You'll be all right. Your concealment is good, and you've learned to move quietly. That's a big step in the right direction. Your marksmanship is fine, and so is your unarmed combat. You'll be all right,' he repeated.

Privately, he wondered why an American outfit with no combat experience at all had been assigned to a covert operation of this importance. They were good fellows, and tough, but it wouldn't do. He made up his mind to ask Masters about it.

'I thought they did very well indeed, Major Douglas,' said a voice from the rear. Douglas swung round and saw Captain DeVine, one hand resting on a tree trunk. He was wearing combat fatigues.

'What are you doing here, Captain?' Douglas asked.

The other smiled. 'Observing,' he said. 'In fact, I've been observing for quite some time. Didn't you see me?'

Implicit in his remark was the responsibility that he could have shot Douglas or any of the SAS team at any moment, had he been an enemy. It was Douglas's turn to feel discomfiture, especially as he noticed broad grins breaking out on the faces of some of the Americans.

'No, I didn't,' Douglas told him, rather truculently. 'I repeat, what are you doing here?'

DeVine gave what amounted to a tolerant smile and looked from Douglas to McCoy. 'Well,' he said, 'I guess now is as good a time as any to tell you. Major McCoy, you'll have been wondering why no other officer has been assigned to your Ranger detachment.'

McCoy nodded. 'It did cross my mind,' he admitted.

'Wonder no longer, sir,' DeVine told him. 'As of this moment, I am your second-in-command.'

'You're my *what*?'

Douglas noticed, with some satisfaction, that the grins had abruptly vanished from the Americans' faces. McCoy looked as though he were about to have an apoplectic fit.

The SAS officer decided that it was time to intervene. 'Gentlemen, perhaps you'd care to join me in a little stroll. The rest of you, take a break for breakfast.'

Accompanied by McCoy and DeVine, Douglas walked some way through the wood until he was out of earshot of the troops. He waited and turned to face DeVine. His face was stern.

'All right,' he said, 'let's get one thing absolutely clear. I am in overall command of this operation, and if a bee so much as farts I want to know about it. I knew nothing about you joining in. Just who the blazes are you, Captain?'

DeVine looked at him and pulled out a pack of cigarettes. He shook one out and lit it, very slowly and deliberately. He replaced the pack in his pocket without offering its contents to anyone else.

'Okay, Major, here it is from the top. I'm oss. You know what that is?'

Douglas did. The Office of Strategic Services was the American equivalent of the British Special Operations Executive. If DeVine had expected Douglas to be impressed by his remark, the man was disappointed. Douglas had dealt with secret agents too many times, had shared too many common dangers with them. His own wife, Colette, had been an SOE agent — safe from the war now, thank God, and ensconced in the family home in Perthshire.

'I suppose that means you know how to handle yourself,' he said. 'Go on.'

DeVine appeared somewhat offended by the other's nonchalant tone.

'Yes, Major, I do know how to handle myself, as you put it. I've qualified as a marksman on all the small arms used by both the Allies and the enemy, I have first-class unarmed combat experience and I have been behind enemy lines three times, operating with Number One Special Force in Italy. I speak fluent German,' he added.

'Well, that's likely to come in handy,' Douglas said. 'What else?'

DeVine took a drag on his cigarette and exhaled the smoke slowly through his nostrils. He parried Douglas's question with one of his own.

'Major, do you have any idea — any idea at all — about what you'll be looking for on the other side?'

'I'm not quite sure that I follow you,' Douglas said. 'The orders seem simple enough. All we have to do is locate the factory making this super-bomb thing and blow it up. Is there something more?'

DeVine nodded. 'Much more, Major. This is not just a question of destroying a few installations. We need to secure all possible information surrounding the German super-bomb project before it falls into — shall I say — other hands. We must, as a matter of urgent priority, round up the scientists who are behind it and bring them out to safety.'

This was news to both Douglas and McCoy. Surprised, the latter asked: 'Why don't we just bump 'em off?'

'Because, Major, we need their services,' DeVine explained. 'If they have already advanced to the point of producing an operational atomic bomb, it means that they can aid us in cutting a few corners. And it's vital that whatever knowledge they possess comes to us, and us alone.'

Douglas looked at him in curiosity. 'What are you frightened of?' he asked abruptly.

'Not what, Major. Whom. The war in Europe is all but wrapped up. Even if the enemy did succeed in using a super-bomb, it would make no difference. We know they don't have the resources to produce more than one such weapon. We have to prevent them from doing that, of course — the loss of life would by truly appalling. But it would make no difference to the outcome of the war here in Europe, except perhaps to increase the bloodiness of its end. There'd be people who would want to show the Germans no mercy.'

He paused and threw down his cigarette, only half smoked in the typical American manner. The others looked at him expectantly.

'We have to look farther afield,' DeVine went on. 'Much farther. There's Japan to contend with, of course, but she can't survive. We don't even need to invade her — we can strangle her to death by blockade if we have to. But when this war is over, what then?'

'We all live happily ever after,' Douglas said sardonically.

'Hardly that, Major. The politics of the world have been turned upside down by this war; when it's over there is likely to be a major upheaval, a struggle for power centred right here in Europe. Whoever comes out on top, it will be the nation with the ability to wield the biggest stick.'

'For stick, read super-bomb,' McCoy said quietly.

'Exactly, Major,' DeVine said. 'Think what the consequences might be if the Russians were to deploy such a weapon first, with German help. It wouldn't take them long to set up the necessary industrial processes, and we know that they have already advanced quite a long way down the path of theoretical atomic physics themselves. I think you know what I'm talking about, Major Douglas.'

Douglas nodded, recalling the events of a year earlier, when the Russians had neatly turned the tables on him after the operation against the German rocket and nerve gas establishment. 'So that's really what this is all about,' he said. 'Well, I'll be damned.'

'We may all be, Major, if the Russians get to those scientists first,' DeVine said ominously. 'Everything else is of secondary importance.'

Douglas was suddenly conscious of the smell of frying bacon and an aroma of coffee drifting through the trees. He looked at DeVine.

'The one thing I really like about you Americans, Captain, is your rations. Let's grab something to eat.' He gave a disarming smile. 'Oh, and by the way — welcome aboard.'

DeVine smiled back. 'Thanks, Major. And I suggest you have a good breakfast. It may be the last cooked one you have for a while.'

Douglas looked at him questioningly. 'Oh. Why's that?'

'Brigadier Masters told me to let you know. We move out tonight.'

*

'Hell, Cal, it seems simple enough to me. All we gotta do is break through the Siegfried Line, avoid being shot or blown up by mines, and then make a sixty-mile forced march through the Black Forest. Easy.' McCoy's tone was sarcastic.

Douglas looked sideways at him. 'You forgot to mention the Rhine,' he reminded the American. 'We've got to get across that first.'

In fact, he knew that the Rhine was likely to prove the least of the obstacles confronting them. The Siegfried Line, with its concrete blockhouses, tank traps and minefields was quite another matter. The only point in their favour was that the fortifications in this sector were comparatively lightly defended; many of the garrison troops had been moved to the northern sector of the Black Forest, where the First French Army of General de Lattre had broken through in the last days of March and then pushed on to Lake Karlsruhe.

Karlsruhe, Douglas reflected, was only fifty miles from Hechingen. The French Army could have pushed on, because the German Nineteenth Army was falling apart rapidly and in many places was reduced to isolated pockets of resistance, but instead the French had been ordered to halt after pushing only twenty miles beyond the Rhine. It failed to make sense — unless the Americans had a good reason for not wanting the French to get to Hechingen and its secrets first.

Well, he'd been deeper than sixty miles into enemy territory before, but to be landed with an operation like this, with all its attendant dangers, and with the war nearly over, seemed a bit unfair. His men thought so too; he could tell that by studying their faces, reddened by the setting sun as the truck rolled southwards from Strasbourg. They were expressionless, and that was a bad sign. They've had enough, he thought wearily. We've all had enough.

Only Stan Brough seemed animated. He was engaged in deep conversation with McCoy's senior NCO a lean and wiry Master Sergeant named Walecki. Brough had discovered, to his great delight, that Walecki had also been a railwayman before the war. They had already swapped enough stories to fill half a book.

Douglas could no longer see his men's faces by the time the truck reached a small village and stopped on the other side. The village, he knew, was called Boofzheim. The Rhine lay some three miles to the east, through woodland. The detailed planning of the operation started to become reality as of now.

'All right, everybody out. Now we start walking. Don't forget the boats.'

He dropped the tailboard of the truck and jumped down, followed by the others. In addition to their personal kit and weaponry they carried five packs containing inflatable rubber boats, each of which could hold four men.

The twenty men of the detachment were wearing their normal British or American battledress. It would be the first time that Douglas's ss men had penetrated deeply into enemy territory without some form of camouflage — either German uniforms or the black one-piece overall specially devised for clandestine operations — but there had been no time to organize it. Neither had there been time to acquire German MP-40 sub-machine-guns, which Douglas preferred for operations inside enemy territory because the 9-mm ammunition they used could be taken from captured enemy stocks. As a consequence, his own men were armed with Sten guns and the Americans with M3 sub-machine-guns. At a pinch the Sten would take German 9-mm ammunition, but the M3, which fired .45 calibre rounds, would not. In addition to his commando knife, each man also carried grenades and some plastic explosive charges. Bill Mitchell carried an extra burden in the form of a radio transceiver, but he was used to that.

Douglas glanced up the road towards the village. There was not a soul to be seen in the rapidly gathering dusk, which he thought strange. This was right in the middle of the French sector, and there ought to have been some sign of their troops somewhere — unless someone at very high level had been pulling some strings to keep his team's departure secure from inquisitive eyes. They had passed plenty of Frenchmen, and German civilians too, at other points during their journey.

The men checked their weapons and equipment. Presently, McCoy came up to Douglas and nodded. 'Okay, Cal. All set.'

They moved off in single file, with Douglas in the lead, across an expanse of flat agricultural land that led to the woods bordering the river. The evening air was cool and pleasant and full of scent. Behind them, the moon, in its first quarter, was brilliant and low in the western sky.

They entered the woods, moving more cautiously now. Douglas thought it highly unlikely that the enemy, desperately short of manpower and in a state of disorganization, might have slipped a patrol across the river in this quiet sector, but one could never tell.

The slope of the ground became progressively steeper, so that they occasionally had to steady themselves by holding on to tree trunks to keep themselves from slipping. Night creatures, startled by their passage, rustled in the bushes on either side.

They could hear the rush of the river now, and soon they arrived at a spot where the woods gave way to an expanse of gravelly bank. Douglas brought them to a halt and went forward alone, crouching among some bushes that bordered the bank while he examined the opposite side through his night glasses. As far as he could tell, the two banks were identical. This was not the Rhine of soaring cliffs and towering fortresses, and for that Douglas was thankful. Whoever had picked this spot for their entry into Germany had known what he was about. Their journey would be tough enough without having to surmount formidable obstacles at its very beginning.

Douglas retreated into the fringe of the woods and addressed the others.

'It seems all quiet,' he said. 'They won't be expecting trouble in this sector. As soon as we get through those woods on the other side, though, we'll hit open ground and the Siegfried Line defences. As you were told at the briefing, the Siegfried Line consists mainly of interconnecting concrete pillboxes, staggered to give defence in depth and with minefields laid out front. Those will be our biggest obstacle. As far as we know there isn't any barbed wire, thank God. Now, you all know the drill for getting through the minefield?'

There were affirmative murmurs in the darkness around him.

'Good. Then let's go. And good luck, everyone. See you in Germany.'

They crept down to the river's edge, where they unpacked and inflated the rubber boats. Douglas pushed out the first one, wading into the river, and climbed in, followed by Barber, Davies and Carter. They unshipped the short paddles and eased their way out into the current. At this point the river was about a quarter of a mile wide and the current, although noticeable, was not sufficiently strong to make paddling a difficult task.

The rush of the water masked all other sounds. Their paddles sliced into the river in unison, pushing the boat steadily onward. Douglas glanced back, and was gratified to discover that he could not see the other boats in the darkness. That meant they would be invisible to anyone on the opposite bank, too.

They reached the far bank in what seemed a surprisingly short time, arriving at a spot where a stunted tree pushed its branches out over the river. Douglas reached up and grabbed one of them, pulling the rubber boat into the bank. He stepped out carefully into knee-deep water, his boots sinking into clinging mud, and hauled himself up on the bank. His companions followed, dragging the boat with them to make way for those coming bchind.

Within five minutes all five boatloads were safely on the bank. Quietly, Douglas ordered some of his men to advance up the slope a few yards to provide a defensive screen while the others deflated the dinghies and deposited them carefully out of sight in the river, weighing them down with rocks.

They were just finishing this task when Olds appeared at Douglas's shoulder. He had been scouting a short distance along the river bank, and returned with the news that he had discovered a gulley that cut through the slope. A stream ran through it, feeding the Rhine.

'Good work, Brian,' Douglas said. 'That's the way we'll go. Pass the word along to wade up through the stream — the sides of the gulley might be mined.'

Olds led them to the stream. Its water swirled around their lower legs as they advanced up the gulley in single file, weapons at the ready. Every now and then they halted, listening for sounds of possible danger, but only the gurgling of the stream broke the silence.

After a few hundred yards the trees on either side of the gulley began to thin out. Douglas called a halt and passed the word down the line for Joe McCoy to join him.

'There's open ground up ahead, Joe,' he whispered. 'Let's go on ahead and see how the land lies.'

The two of them went on alone. Presently, the slope became less pronounced and the ground progressively more boggy. It was now clear that the little stream had its origin in a marshy area where the land flattened out at the top of the slope. The fact was to their advantage; it was impossible to lay mines in marshy ground.

Douglas got out his binoculars and scanned the terrain ahead, the light-gathering lenses making it possible to pick out features in extraordinary detail. After a minute or two he handed the glasses to McCoy.

'Take a good look,' he whispered. 'We've got to cross about a mile of flat ground before we reach more cover. You can see the forest edge quite clearly. There are blockhouses, too, on both right and left flanks — but none immediately in front of us. See what I mean?'

'Yeah. Must mean that this swampy ground cuts right across. This is a damn good place to go over, Cal. Wonder if our people knew about it? They didn't mention it at the briefing.'

Douglas did not speculate. Instead, he said: 'Well, we might as well get on with it. We'll go across in single file. I'll lead. If we run into trouble and anything happens to me, don't hesitate, Joe — get the chaps back to the river as fast as you can. Once the Huns know we're here we might as well pack up and go home. Understood?'

McCoy nodded in the darkness. 'Okay, Cal. Fingers crossed.'

They went back down the gulley and briefed the others on what lay ahead. Everyone checked his webbing and equipment to ensure that there would be no metallic sounds to give away their presence. If they were detected, Douglas knew, it would be by accident or by sound.

Douglas led the way into the marsh, walking in a semi-crouched position as he placed one foot carefully in front of the other. His boots made muted squelching noises as he pulled them free with each step. In places, his feet sank in the mire up to his ankles. He found himself hoping fervently that the bog would not become impassable, and had a sudden vision of a childhood nightmare in which he was trying to escape from some unseen horror but could not, because his feet were weighed down.

The dark, squat shapes of the blockhouses were visible now to the unaided eye. The nearest ones were, perhaps, a couple of hundred yards distant on either side. He forced himself to concentrate on following a course that would take him and his men right between them — a difficult process, because as yet he was unable to fix on any reference point ahead of him.

The squelching of his boots suddenly seemed unnaturally loud. He resisted a wild desire to try and move faster and realized that he had subconsciously been counting the steps ever since he had set off. It was an old habit, and a useful one when crossing open ground. It told you how far you were from cover.

His mental counter told him now that they must have reached the half way point. The point of no return. He was soaked in sweat. Keep going, he told himself. One foot in front of the other. Keep going, counting all the time.

Suddenly, his boots were no longer squelching in mud. He brushed perspiration from his eyes, searching ahead of him, and was conscious that the ground was rising. Coarse grass brushed his legs. He glanced back; the blockhouses were no longer visible in the darkness. He sucked in a long breath of relief.

There were trees ahead, sheltering trees where they could rest for a few moments and pull their nerves together. They were through the Siegfried Line, and thanks to the bog they had made the crossing in record time.

Wearily, he leaned against the trunk of a tree and waited for the others to join him. He longed for a cigarette, but that was out of the question. He was shaking all over.

Liam Conolly came and stood beside him. 'Jesus, Boss,' the Irishman said, 'my nerves are shot to hell. I don't want to do that again in a hurry.'

Somehow, the words made Douglas feel better. He took a deep breath and managed to shrug off some of the strain.

'Could have been worse, Liam. We might have had to crawl through a minefield.'

He inspected the luminous dial of his watch. 'Five minutes, that's all. Then we're on our way again. We've a long way to travel before dawn.'

CHAPTER SIX

No one except those who needed to know had ever heard of Base w-47. Its real name was Wendover Field, and it lay in a desolate, barren wilderness one hundred and twenty-five miles west of Salt Lake City in the Utah Desert. It was as remote from civilization as the moon, and ideal for the 509th Bombardment Group's top-secret purpose.

Base w-47 was home to fifteen hundred personnel, drawn from bases scattered all over the world. Many of them had been selected personally by Colonel Paul Tibbetts, the 509th Group's commander.

At twenty-nine years of age, Tibbetts was recognized as one of the most experienced bomber pilots in the USAAF. He had flown B-17s on operations over Europe for nearly eighteen months before returning to the United States in 1944 to play a leading part in the operational development of the B-29 Superfortress, the big four-engined bomber that was to form the keystone of America's strategic bombing offensive against Japan.

It was in August 1944 that Tibbetts had received an urgent telephone call ordering him to report immediately to General Uzal Ent, commanding the USAAF Strategic Forces HQ at Colorado Springs. There, Tibbetts had met Dr Norman Ramsey, a Harvard professor and a specialist in ballistics research, and Captain William Parsons, chief of weapons development under a scientist named Dr Robert Oppenheimer at a remote research establishment in the New Mexico Desert: Los Alamos.

It had taken Ramsey and Parsons a week to turn Tibbetts into a scientist. In a briefing that lasted several days he was initiated into the mysteries of nuclear physics, of the splitting of the atom and the undreamed-of energies that were released as a result. He was told as much as he needed to know about Project Manhattan, the biggest scientific research programme ever undertaken by mankind, of the efforts of thousands of scientists and engineers all channelled towards one goal: the production of the most awesome weapon in the history of warfare, the atomic bomb.

Tibbetts was not slow to grasp the enormity of what he heard, or of the task that lay ahead of him. No one yet knew whether the weapon would work, but if it did it would have to be delivered to an enemy target. That was Tibbetts' job: to form a special bombardment group composed of the best air and ground crews the USAAF had to offer and train them to an unparalleled standard of skill and accuracy. The programme was known as Operation Silver Plate.

By the end of September 1944 Tibbetts had succeeded in bringing the 509th Bombardment Group to strength, with its full complement of officers and enlisted men and fourteen new B-29S. The group was a fully self-contained unit, and security precautions were stringent in the extreme; FBI agents with top security ratings shadowed personnel in their off-duty spells and reported any irregularities they overheard.

The element of the 509th Group which would deliver the actual weapon to its as yet unspecified target was the 393rd Bombardment Squadron, which was well into an intensive training programme by October 1944. None of the crews had the remotest idea of what their eventual task was to be and there was widespread puzzlement over the nature of the training, which involved a weapon delivery technique totally different from anything previously employed.

Bombing practice, carried out over remote desert areas of the United States, always involved a run-in to the target — a white circle on the ground — at altitudes of not less than thirty thousand feet. Great emphasis was placed on achieving the maximum visual bombing accuracy, something else that perplexed the bombardiers; over Europe weather conditions had led to the development of radar bombing techniques, and the weather was likely to be even worse over Japan.

In December 1944 the 393rd Squadron moved to Cuba, where it was to spend eight weeks. From here, the crews practised long-range sorties over the ocean, a sure indication that they would eventually move to the Pacific.

Meanwhile, development of the Allied atomic bomb was proceeding at a fast rate, and by the end of December 1944 Brigadier-General Leslie Groves, in overall command of the project, felt confident enough to announce a timetable. In a memorandum to the us Chief of Staff, General George Marshall, he indicated that the first operational atomic bomb ought to be ready by the first day of August 1945. He suggested that the

Pacific Naval Command be alerted and a base set up for the 509th Group from which its B-29S could reach Japanese targets.

Two months later Commander Fred Ashworth, who had been in charge of ballistics development at Wendover, flew to Guam to see Admiral Chester Nimitz, the us Navy c-in-c Pacific. Ashworth carried a letter signed by Admiral Ernest King, Chief of Naval Operations, which explained the atomic bomb project and requested that Ashworth be given the highest priority in his mission.

The base selected by Ashworth was Tinian, in the Marianas, a hundred miles nearer to Japan than Guam. A level limestone platform some six miles wide by thirteen in length, Tinian's very smallness made it ideal for the secret nature of the undertaking. Moreover, it had a network of good roads developed by the Japanese, and plans were already afoot to turn the island's North Field air base, with its four concrete runways, into the biggest bomber base in the world.

While hordes of us Navy engineers worked flat out to transform Tinian into an unsinkable aircraft carrier, development of the Allied atomic bomb picked up speed in the spring of 1945, with the reactors at Oak Ridge and Hanford already producing uranium 235 and plutonium in small quantities. The designs of the first two atomic bombs were also being finalized; the uranium bomb was nicknamed 'Thin Man' after President Roosevelt, while the more bulky plutonium bomb was named 'Fat Man' after Winston Churchill.

In March 1945 the 393rd Squadron returned from Cuba to Wendover for more trials over the deserts of the western United States. The bombs they used this time featured the finalized design, weighing a little over four and a half tons with charges of high explosive, and the fall of each missile was recorded by cameras and scientists who accompanied every training mission.

The training was still in progress when General Groves visited Wendover at the end of the first week of April. He had grim news to impart to Paul Tibbetts.

Groves' c-47 transport was surrounded by armed guards as soon as it taxied to a stop, and a pair of FBI agents escorted the general to Tibbetts' office. Tibbetts, with no foreknowledge of the general's visit, was absent on a training mission. Groves, armed with his third cup of coffee, watched the return of the silver B-29 through the colonel's office window and saw the crew disembark.

Tibbetts' face betrayed no surprise when he found Groves waiting for him. The general was in the habit of dropping in from time to time, to check on progress. The two men shook hands warmly.

'Well, Paul,' Groves said. 'How's it all going?'

'Fine, sir. We've got the aiming problems sorted out, and we can put the practice bombs slap in the circle every time. Some of the guys are getting a bit edgy, though — they'd dearly like to know what the end product will be.' He suddenly noticed the serious expression on Groves' face, and asked if anything was wrong. Groves nodded slowly.

'Yes, Paul, there is. Very much so. To put it bluntly, the Germans have cut some corners in their atomic research programme. It's pretty certain that they've caught up with us — in fact, they might even be ahead of us.'

Tibbetts' face took on an incredulous expression. 'You mean — they might actually be building a bomb? Right now?'

Groves nodded again. 'That's it, Paul. Their operation at Hechingen was bigger, much bigger, than we imagined. And they've got other research sites in the area.'

He paused for a moment, then asked: 'Paul, if you were the enemy, and had the operational atomic bomb tomorrow, how would you use it?'

Tibbetts pondered the question, his brow furrowed. 'Well,' he said at length, 'I'd go for the biggest target available. The one that would produce the biggest impact. London, say, or maybe Moscow. No, on reflection I'd make it London. Easier to reach with what they've got available. I've seen the photos of those modified Heinkels — they could reach London all right.'

Groves looked the pilot straight in the eye 'There's another possibility, Paul. What would you say if I suggested the Germans might be going for New York?'

Tibbetts shook his head. 'Quite out of the question, sir. They've nothing with that kind of range. If they had, they'd have bombed New York long before now.'

Groves raised an eyebrow, then turned aside and delved into his briefcase. He produced a photograph and showed it to Tibbetts. It was the air reconnaissance shot of the Junkers 390 on the ground at Rechlin. He described the aircraft briefly.

'That's quite capable of reaching New York, Paul. Maybe not from Germany, but from a base in Norway. With a bomb weighing five or six tons it might be a one-way trip, but it would get there. A Superfort has a range of three thousand miles, and that bird's a lot bigger.'

Tibbetts scratched his head. 'Norway, you say?'

'That's right. They're up to something there. During the past few weeks there's been a big movement of troops to Norway from the Baltic ports. Aircraft, too. So why would they move forces to Norway when their whole situation in Germany is collapsing? It can only be because they're planning some sort of last stand there, and there'd be no point in that unless they believe they can still turn on us in some way. And that means the bomb.'

'But I don't follow how this ties in with their operation at Hechingen,' Tibbetts objected. 'Presumably that's where they're building their bomb. But that whole area is likely to be overrun in a couple of weeks or less. Why didn't they just shift the whole operation to Norway?'

'Too late for that, Paul,' Groves said. 'They could have done that a couple of years ago, but they learned we were on to them — remember the commando raid on the heavy water plant at Vemork? That's when they decided to base their atomic research centre in southern Germany. Now, I'd like you to take a look at something else.'

He took two more air reconnaissance photographs from his briefcase and showed them to the pilot, who examined them closely. They were dated, and there was a month between them. A feature at the centre of each photograph was marked by a white arrow. Both photographs depicted a broad valley that lay between two areas of wooded high ground to the south of Hechingen. On the first photograph, the arrow pointed towards what appeared to be nothing more than an expanse of agricultural land. On the second -

'Hey, that's interesting!' Tibbetts exclaimed. 'There's some sort of line feature here, extending out into the valley. Looks as though it starts in those woods there. Must be over a mile long. It's a bit vague, but it definitely doesn't show in the earlier photograph,'

'That's because it's just been built, Paul,' Groves told him. 'As you've probably guessed, it's an airstrip. It's very well camouflaged, but not quite well enough.'

The pieces of the jigsaw puzzle were beginning to fit together in Tibbetts' mind.

'So that's it.' He handed the photographs back to Groves. 'They're assembling the bomb components at Hechingen, or somewhere in the vicinity, and then flying them out to Norway.'

'That's if they've started,' Groves said. 'We're working on the assumption that they haven't. We've infiltrated a strong sabotage team composed of some of our Rangers and some British Special Air Service men into the Hechingen area — at least, they're on their way. We hope they can nip this thing in the bud before it gets really dangerous.'

Groves turned and stared out of the window, his eyes following a B-29 which was just lifting up from the runway.

'If they can't, Paul — well, let's do some imagining. The Germans use their bomb, maybe against New York, maybe not. My guess it will be New York, because once they've bombed that with their long-range bird they've got other airplanes capable of attacking London and Moscow-those modified Heinkels, for instance. You know about them.'

Tibbetts nodded. He had been well briefed on what the Allies knew about the enemy's atomic research effort. He waited for Groves to continue.

'So they bomb New York,' the general went on, 'and the war in Europe comes to a standstill. We think they've only got the resources to build one bomb, but we don't know for sure. Can you imagine how the politicians would react?

There would be a stalemate in Europe, terror — maybe panic — in London and Moscow. God knows, their people have suffered enough already, especially the British. How would the politicians and the generals say to them, 'Okay, we go on fighting — but you must expect to be obliterated at any moment if we do?'

'But what would they achieve by it?' Tibbetts asked. 'The Germans, I mean? They must have an inkling that we're building the bomb too, and that when we both have it we'll be back to square one.'

The general turned back from the window to face him. 'They're desperate people, Paul. They know that they can't prevent us from building our own bomb. What they *can* do is buy time — maybe force us into an armistice with them, so that they can turn on the Russians.'

Groves paused for a few moments, then said, 'You asked what would happen if those commandos failed in their mission, Paul. Well, here it is, straight down the line. If they succeed, you will deploy to Tinian in a few days' time and proceed with the mission against Japan. But if they fail —

'

He walked over to a map of the world that was pinned to the wall. 'If they fail, you will await orders to deploy to Europe, to a base in the British Isles. There, you will be assigned a new target. I can tell you right now what that target will be.'

His finger hovered over the map for a moment, then came to rest on the city of Berlin.

CHAPTER SEVEN

A dense fog had rolled down the valleys of the Black Forest during the night, and by daybreak it had crept up the slopes to hang in tendrils among the trees, causing the trunks to glisten with moisture. It blotted out everything more than a few yards away, deadening all sound and providing a welcome cloak of camouflage for those who, for one reason or another, did not wish to be seen.

In one forest clearing, a thousand feet above the adjacent valley, wisps of smoke curled from a small fire, mingling with the surrounding fog. On a makeshift spit above the flame a roasting pheasant hissed and crackled. Two more birds, already plucked, lay nearby. The fog had made the birds stupid and disorientated, and it had been an easy matter to knock them off the lower branches of the tree where they had been roosting, waiting for the sun to filter through.

Three men sat round the fire, warming their hands at the little flame. Their faces were gaunt and they eyed the roasting meat hungrily, spittle drooling from the corners of their mouths.

For coats they wore threadbare blankets, with holes cut for their arms and heads. The blankets did not conceal the striped rags that formed the rest of their clothing, the rags of slave labourers and concentration camp inmates.

Suddenly, one of the men lunged forward and seized the roasting bird. He tore a leg from it and handed it to the man next to him, who took his own share before passing it on. They ate like animals, tearing at the barely cooked meat, yet without selfishness; each took his fair share and no more. They could afford to take their time over the second pheasant and eat it with more appreciation, once their initial hunger pains had been dulled.

A twig cracked. The little tableau by the fire froze into still life. Only the eyes of the men moved, seeking to penetrate the fog and to locate the source of the sound.

After a few moments the man who had been chewing on the leg of the pheasant let its remains fall to the ground. Slowly he stood up, his chin raised, nostrils narrowed as he sniffed the damp air. He could smell wet wool mixed with something else, the acrid aroma of stale tobacco clinging to a man's clothing.

There were shadows in the fog, approaching the fire from different directions. The men in the striped rags watched helplessly, knowing that it was useless to try and run. The clearing was surrounded. Perhaps surrounded was the right word, for only half a dozen men were approaching slowly through the trees, but that was enough. Already, the fugitives could see that they carried guns.

The man who had been eating the pheasant's leg felt like weeping. They had done so well to come this far since escaping from the work party a week ago. Now it was over. He knew that they would die here in this clearing, shot down like dogs.

The men with the guns stopped a few yards away. Their leader pointed his carbine at the standing fugitive, whose name was Anton. The latter saw now that the men were *Volkssturm*, the German home guard. They were middle aged, and one or two were even elderly. Anton felt a sudden flicker of hope; he had heard that many of the *Volkssturm* no longer had any stomach for the war, now that of necessity they had been turned into full-time soldiers to undertake guard duties in Germany as the younger men were sent to the front.

Perhaps, thought Anton wildly, they will let us go. After all, the war is nearly over. What difference would it make?

His hopes were brutally dashed. The *Volkssturm* leader, a big man with piggy eyes and a flattened nose, glared at him and spat on the ground. His gun menaced Anton's chest.

'Scum!' he snarled. 'You've led us a merry dance! Well, now you're going to pay for it. Stand up, you two, and get your hands in the air. If you have a God, you'd better start praying to him.'

The other two fugitives rose and stood beside Anton, their faces filled with misery and despair.

'We don't even have the chance to die with our bellies full,' one of them muttered.

Anton looked at him. 'I'm sorry,' he said. 'I'm truly sorry. We should have stayed at the camp. We might have survived then, until the Allies arrived.'

In his heart he knew that that would not have been the case. It was common knowledge that all the camp inmates were destined to be shot out of hand, once their task was done.

'No talking!' the *Volkssturm* man snapped. He barked out an order to his men, who also pointed their guns at the fugitives. One or two of the barrels wavered a little.

'Franz, is this really necessary?' one of the elderly part-time soldiers complained. 'Can't we just take them prisoner and hand them over? I'd rather someone else did the dirty work.'

'Bah, you gutless old bastard! Go away and chew the cud. I'll finish the job myself!'

He raised the carbine to his shoulder and took careful aim at Anton's chest. The fugitive did not close his eyes; instead he stared over the German's head at the moisture-laden branches of a tree. He had always loved trees, and now the sight of one would be his last vision on earth.

He heard a swishing noise, and wondered vaguely what it could be. Then came another sound, a metallic clatter. He dropped his gaze from the tree and looked at the *Volkssturm* soldier. The man was staring back at him, his eyes wide. He had dropped his carbine. How could that possibly be? Anton wondered. Then he saw the knife, protruding from the side of the German's neck.

The German's hand fluttered and he gave a choking grunt of surprise. Blood welled from his mouth. He pitched forward like a felled tree and hit the ground facedown with a thud.

Anton could not yet comprehend what was happening. Swift, spectral shapes materialized from the fog and closed with the other *Volkssturm* men. Later, Anton could not remember having heard the slightest sound. It was like watching frames from a silent movie.

Within seconds, the Germans lay dead on the forest floor.

A tall man in military uniform approached him. He was followed by others, all of them heavily armed. The tall man said something to him in a language he did not understand. Anton looked him up and down. Suddenly, recognition dawned. He sank to his knees, sobbing, and tried to seize the man's hand. The soldier, clearly embarrassed, pulled back hastily.

'*Les anglais,*' Anton whispered through his tears. '*Ils sont arrivés. Les alliés sont arrives! Nous sommes sauvés!*'

'Oh, hell,' Douglas swore. 'Liam, find out who these fellows are, will you? The rest of you, dispose of that lot, will you?' He indicated the dead Germans. 'Cover 'em up well. We don't want anyone tripping over them just yet.'

Inwardly, Douglas was cursing himself. He should have let the Germans shoot these poor wretches while he and his men slipped quietly by. At the same time, he knew in his heart that he could not have stood by and allowed such a thing to happen.

Conolly went up to Anton and questioned him. Presently, he nodded and returned to Douglas. There was a look of satisfaction on his face.

'They're Belgians,' he said, 'and this could be a lucky break for us. They're forced labourers, and they've been working on various sites at Hechingen. They know the place inside out. They managed to escape a few days ago, and have been on the run ever since. Poor beggars, they look half-starved.'

'Well, give them some rations,' Douglas ordered, 'and ask them if they know what's going on at Hechingen.'

'I already have asked them, and they've no idea,' Conolly informed him. 'This chap tells me they've been building some sort of underground hangar in the side of the valley, and an airstrip to go with it. It was finished a day or two before these three escaped. And guess what?'

'What?' Douglas looked at him impatiently.

'The Germans flew an aircraft in as soon as the job was completed. According to this bloke, it didn't have any propellers and made a funny whistling noise. He got a pretty good look at it, too.'

Douglas thought furiously and beckoned to Joe McCoy, who had been supervising the disposal of the Germans. He explained what they had learned so far from the Belgian.

'A jet airplane,' McCoy said.

'That could be important.' The speaker was Captain DeVine, who had also joined them and overheard their conversation, i know a little about these jets of theirs. If we could find out what kind it was, maybe it would tell us a little more about what the Germans intend to do. Did you say that Belgian guy got a good look at it?'

Douglas nodded. 'Feel free to ask him some questions,' he said.

'Thanks. I will.' DeVine went over to Anton and spoke to him at some length, sketching something deftly in a little notebook as he did so. The

Belgian shook his head from time to time, indicating that the American was to make some alteration to his drawing. After a few minutes DeVine rejoined the other officers.

'There's no doubt about it,' he told them, 'It's an Arado 234, a jet bomber. It's my guess that the Germans are using it to ferry materials and possibly personnel into and out of the Hechingen site at night. The Arado is too fast for any of our fighters to catch.'

The significance of what DeVine was saying was not lost on Douglas.

'Correct me if I'm wrong,' he said. 'This what d'you call it — this Arado is probably being used to ferry whatever the Germans are producing at Hechingen to some other location. Now, where would that be, I wonder?'

'One thing's for sure,' McCoy said, 'it has to be somewhere outside Germany. Germany isn't big enough any longer to warrant a special jet plane being laid on as a transport. Anybody know how far this thing can fly?'

'Well,' DeVine said, 'our technical people were able to examine one last month, when it crash-landed behind our lines after an attack on the bridge we'd captured at Remagen, over the Rhine. I saw the report. A preliminary assessment suggested that the Arado will fly around seven hundred miles. Enough to take it as far as England, or Denmark, without refuelling. But then, we're just speculating, aren't we?'

Yet again, Douglas had a deep suspicion that the enigmatic DeVine knew more than he was prepared to admit. He changed the subject.

'I was just thinking,' he said, 'that these Belgian chaps could be a great deal of use to us if we can persuade them to go back to Hechingen. They look about all in, but we've only got about twenty miles to go. We'll carry them if we have to. After all, Liam, you said they knew the place inside out. Might make life a lot easier.'

Conolly nodded. 'Good idea, Boss. I'll have a word.'

He went back and spoke to Anton, who at first shook his head vehemently. After a couple of minutes the Belgian conferred with his two colleagues, then allowed himself to be led across to where Douglas was waiting.

'He's not happy,' Conolly said, 'but he'll come with us. The other two won't, though. They say they're going to hide in the forest until the war's over. Can't say I blame them,' he added.

Douglas pondered. 'I don't like it,' he said. 'If they get caught they'll probably give the game away. Still, we can't force the poor beggars. They've been through enough, by the look of things. Tell them to get well away from here, though — those Huns we did in will be missed before long.'

He turned to Anton and thanked him in a few words of schoolboy French. The man smiled at him, a little sadly, and gave an expressive shrug. Douglas realized that under the dirt and the rags, Anton was quite young, probably no more than twenty-five. He certainly looked fitter than his two friends.

The Americans had made a thorough search of the dead Germans, stripping the bodies of their greatcoats in the process. Douglas bent down, picked one up and handed it to Anton, who accepted it with a smile of gratitude and shed his dirty blanket. Douglas also gave him a German carbine — a Mauser 98 of 1914 — 18 War vintage — and a couple of pouches of ammunition. The man indicated that he knew how to use the gun.

The Americans finished their task of burying the Germans in shallow graves and carefully camouflaged each one. They also dug a hole and buried the remaining rifles and other odds and ends.

Douglas and McCoy looked around, satisfying themselves that the debris of the brief one-sided fight were thoroughly concealed, and Douglas ordered the detachment to move out. As he left the clearing he looked back, and saw that the other two fugitives had been fitted out with German greatcoats, too. Anton embraced each man briefly then ran to catch up with the column. His two companions stared after him, clutching their pheasants and looking dejected. The thought struck Douglas that if the men were captured now, wearing articles of German uniform, it would go hard with them before a bullet ended their lives. It was too late to worry about that now.

We've been lucky so far, Douglas thought. Very lucky. He was right. The weather had been on their side in the two days they'd been on the march since crossing the Rhine, with fog and drizzle covering this area of the Black Forest.

The going had been tough, but not as tough as Douglas had imagined it would be. The forest tracks had led them steadily eastwards, and the only people they had glimpsed, in periods when the weather lifted, had been at a distance; old men and women working in the fields that covered the green, picture-postcard valleys below their line of march. The Black Forest was not the dark, forbidding place Douglas had imagined; it was a wilderness, certainly, but one that had been progressively tamed by two thousand years of human endeavour.

What had astonished him had been the sheer emptiness of the place. He had fully expected to encounter enemy patrols, but — apart from the chance encounter with the luckless *Volkssturm* men — there had been none. There had been plenty of enemy transport moving through the valleys, but the forest itself did not appear to be patrolled — another indication, he thought, of Germany's desperate manpower shortage.

He calculated that he and his men were progressing at a steady mile and a half every hour, resting for ten minutes at two-hourly intervals. They were showing signs of tiredness now, but that was to be expected. At every halt Douglas checked their position carefully; they were now a few miles south of the town of Lossburg, having made good progress in the previous night.

But they still had to face the tricky part. Soon they would emerge from the mountainous area of the Black Forest and enter a region of agricultural lowland. There would be woods there to shelter them, but they must unavoidably cross large tracts of open land. They would have to cover the last fifteen miles to their objective under cover of darkness, facing increasing danger as they got closer to the restricted zone. Even now, Douglas noted as he marched on, the ground was gradually beginning to slope down towards the plain that lay to the east. There were still plenty of bridges to be crossed.

Several hours later, from the shelter of a small copse a few miles north of the little town of Oberndorf, Douglas and McCoy surveyed one of those bridges through their binoculars. It spanned the valley of the river Neckar near the village of Sulz. A road and railway line ran parallel to the Neckar, following the river's west bank. Sentries were clearly visible, patrolling the bridge, and there were armoured vehicles in the nearby village.

'That's the way we have to go, Joe,' Douglas said. 'It'll be tricky, but any other route would take us over much more open ground. Once we've crossed the Neckar, a couple of miles will see us in good cover again.'

McCoy nodded. 'Yeah. Pity the fog's lifted, though; I guess we'll have to wait for nightfall now.'

Douglas swept his binoculars from left to right, imprinting the lie of the land in his mind. He pointed. 'Look, that's where we'll cross. You see that rocky outcrop about half a mile to the right of the village? It looks to me as though it juts out over the river. It'll give us some cover, at least. I wish I could see how steep the sides of the river gorge are, though.'

'Well, we'll find out soon enough,' McCoy said. 'I guess all we can do now is wait.'

Douglas glanced at his watch. It was set to Greenwich Mean Time, and the hands showed that it was 6 p. m. It would be a good hour before sunset, and although the overcast sky would help darkness to come a little sooner, Douglas decided to add on another hour before they moved off.

'Two hours from now, Joe,' he said. 'Time to grab a bite to eat, and a little rest. It might be the last we'll get for some time.'

*

Volksgrenadier Klaus Dreidorfer paced up and down the bridge at Sulz, growing increasingly impatient. That old fool Eickner, his relief, had not yet turned up, and if he didn't get away soon he would be in big trouble with his girl. He had arranged to meet her by the river after dark, as soon as she could slip away from her old man's farm, but she had said that she had no intention of waiting for him. As it was, he'd have to run like hell.

Damn Eickner! The old bastard must be seventy if he was a day, and the upper age limit for the *Volksgrenadiers* was sixty. He should have joined the *Volkssturm*, and kept out of everyone's way. Why, there was no disgrace in that; they even issued the part-timers with proper uniforms in this part of Germany.

And this was likely to be the most important night in seventeen-year-old Dreidorfer's life. The night when Gisela, a couple of years older, had promised to let him go all the way. If he missed his chance, he swore to God he'd kill Eickner and dump him in the river. Nobody would miss the bloody old coffin-maker.

A whiff of ersatz tobacco caught his nostrils and he swung round in alarm. The stooped figure of Eickner was standing there, surrounded by a halo of smoke that issued from a cherry wood pipe.

'Where the hell have you been grandpa?' Dreidorfer snapped. 'And what do you mean by creeping up on a fellow like that?'

'All right, all right,' the old man said condescendingly. 'I'm here now. Some sentry you'd make. If I'd been an enemy, you'd be dead. Go on, go off to your screwing. I know what you're up to. Just hope to God her old man doesn't find out, that's all. Still,' he added as an afterthought, 'you might as well have your turn at her before the Amis or the Ivans get here.'

'You old sod,' the young man snarled. 'I ought to smack you in the teeth. But then, you don't have any, do you? And don't you know it's forbidden to smoke on duty?' Eickner leaned back against the parapet of the bridge and watched Klaus trot off into the darkness. He continued to puff on his pipe, and wondered idly how long it would be before the Americans arrived, so that he could go back to his carpenter's shop and live out the rest of his life in peace. He had fought in one war, and been wounded too; he had not expected to be dragged into another.

'Balls to everything,' he said moodily, and spat into the river.

Klaus Dreidorfer made his way as fast as he could along the bank of the Neckar, stumbling every now and then in his eagerness to be at the rendezvous on time. After a few hundred metres he was forced to climb higher as the river gorge deepened; now at least the path was level and unobstructed by rocks, so that he could run faster.

Gisela was waiting for him where she had said she would be, at a spot where three trees formed an isolated triangle. She admonished him for being late. He noted the annoyance in her voice, and put his arms around her lovingly. She smelled faintly of the cow byre, but he didn't care. He buried his face in her straw-coloured hair.

'It was that fool Eickner,' he explained, his voice muffled. 'Thank you for waiting, *liebchen*. I was so worried.'

She sniffed. 'Well, we don't have much time. I have to be back at the farm soon. *Vati* will kill me if he finds out I've been with you. Come along, over here. And for heaven's sake take off that ridiculous helmet.'

She took him by the hand and led him to a spot in the lee of some bushes. He saw that she had brought a blanket with her, and now she spread it on the damp grass. She sank down on it and reached up, pulling him down beside her. He hastily laid his helmet and rifle to one side.

She deftly began to unfasten the buttons of his tunic. Her hand slid inside and she began to caress his chest. Bolts of lightning seemed to sweep through him. He kissed her wildly, pawing at her breast with one hand and striving to unfasten his trousers with the other. She chuckled in his ear.

'Gently, gently,' she admonished. 'And don't try to undress me — it's too chilly.'

His hand groped downwards and found the hem of her dress. He pulled it up and inserted his hand between her thighs, realizing with a shock that she wore no underwear. Her own hand had somehow found its way into his trousers and she was pulling at his underpants, which had become entangled with his erection. She got him free at last and spread her legs wide apart, guiding him towards her. Her hand was cool upon him. He felt the wetness of her and thrust desperately as he tried to enter her.

'Now,' she gasped, 'now!'

He gave a low, despairing moan and slumped on top of her. She did not need to ask what had happened, for she could feel his hot fluid on her thighs. She struggled out from under him and cupped his face in her hands.

'Never mind,' she said softly. 'Never mind. Just take it easy. You'll be all right again in a few minutes. It'll be fine then.'

He sat up miserably beside her, his head bowed. He mumbled some sort of apology. She chuckled again. 'Silly boy! Do you think you're the first one that's happened to? It happens to most men on their first time, although they'd never admit it. Don't be disappointed. As I said, it'll be —'

Suddenly she was on her back again, his hand clamped over her mouth. She struggled, fear gripping her. Klaus's lips were close to her ear. She wanted to cry out, but could not.

'Lie still!' he whispered urgently. 'It's all right, just lie still and don't move. I heard something over there. Keep very quiet!'

Carefully, he removed his hand. He was fumbling in the darkness beside her, and she sensed that he was fastening his pants. She was suddenly very afraid, not of Klaus but of whatever might be out there.

They lay side by side in the shelter of the bushes and strained their eyes, striving to penetrate the darkness. She could hear it now, too-the swish of boots, moving through grass. There was a smell, too, borne on the night air, the smell of bodies, of sweat.

Klaus pressed her down, a protective arm about her. Their eyes widened as a shadowy figure moved across their line of vision, only a matter of yards away. It was followed by another, and another. Even in darkness, Klaus could see that the men carried guns and wore packs on their backs. He counted twenty-one of them.

The last one vanished into the night. Beside Klaus, Gisela shivered with fear. They lay immobile for several more minutes, just to make sure that there were no more strangers.

'They must have come from the west, from across the river,' Klaus whispered. 'Come — we must report this immediately.'

His companion gave a stifled wail. 'But I can't go with you,' she objected. 'I'll get into terrible trouble.'

He sat up and seized her shoulders roughly. 'Look, this could be important. Those men could be saboteurs, or enemy paratroops, or anything. It's our duty to report what we've just seen. Come along, now!' Suddenly, the boy was in complete command of the situation.

Fifteen minutes later he was standing rigidly to attention in the guard post at Sulz, gasping out his tale to the guard commander. Gisela, hovering behind him, nodded frantically as he spoke, confirming the truth of his statements.

The guard commander stared at him for long moments, taking in the boy's earnest face. His gaze switched to the girl, who was clasping and unclasping her hands in terror of what might happen to her when she got home.

The guard commander made up his mind. He barked out an order, and an NCO who had been standing by the door rushed off and pulled a switch set into the wall. The harsh wail of a siren rent the air, and the entire garrison of Sulz came tumbling from their quarters.

'God help you both,' the guard commander said menacingly, 'if this turns out to be a wild goose chase.'

A mile beyond the river, Douglas and the others also heard the siren, and wondered what it might signify.

CHAPTER EIGHT

The cavern was as big as a barn, and just as draughty. It had been hollowed out of the side of a hill, and an aura of earthy dampness still hung around it. Dim lighting only served to enhance the overall gloomy effect.

Helmut Winter stood on a platform that had been raised at one end of the cavern and shivered, not entirely because of the damp atmosphere. The old terror of being entombed alive was strong inside him, and it was only with great reluctance that he had accepted Skorzeny's invitation to witness the forthcoming scientific experiment.

Skorzeny was now engaged in animated conversation with a small group of his ss subordinates, and had left Winter and Franz Warsitz in the care of Professor Werner Melzer, the young scientist who had recently arrived from Berlin to take charge of the research programme. Melzer now looked at Winter and smiled.

'Well, Major, what do you think of it?'

Winter stared at the massive contraption that dominated the centre of the cavern. He didn't know what to make of it all, and said so.

Melzer chuckled. 'I can't say I blame you for being mystified,' he said. 'However, I understand you've had a little basic instruction in nuclear physics over the past day or two?'

Winter nodded. His head was still reeling with the intricacies of neutrons, isotopes, uranium and the like. He had to admit that Warsitz, with a far more scientific turn of mind, had been much quicker to grasp what it was all about.

'Well then, Major, what you are looking at is an atomic pile. People have been working night and day for months to build this one. It will be far more efficient than the primitive machine at Haigerloch.'

Winter had seen that one, too, during his tour of the area. Germany's first atomic fission experiments had been carried out in an old wine-cellar hewn out of solid rock at the base of a cliff in the little Swabian village of Haigerloch, ten miles west of Hechingen. In the middle of this underground laboratory, a large alloy vessel had been lowered into a water-filled pit. The vessel was lined with ten tons of graphite blocks, leaving a central cavity for the magnesium-alloy vessel in which the atomic reaction was to take place. The vessel's lid was also filled with graphite and sandwiched between magnesium plates; from the lid were suspended seventy-eight chains of uranium cubes.

Success had come one day in December 1944, after months of failure. Before an anxious group of assembled scientists, the graphite lid and chains of uranium cubes had been lowered into place inside the reactor vessel and the lid bolted into place. Then water was pumped into the pit, the neutron source, radium-beryllium, was lowered into the heart of the pile, and one and a half tons of deuterium oxide — heavy water — was slowly pumped in.

As the heavy water reached further and further up the inside of the cylinder, the neutrons, unable to escape because of the graphite shielding, began to multiply rapidly — and suddenly the German scientists achieved the break-through already made by Enrico Fermi in the United States two years earlier. The pile suddenly began to produce energy independent of the neutron source at its centre. The critical point had been reached, and the door to Germany's bomb had been opened.

Now Winter was to witness a similar experiment, but one that would take place with the help of much more advanced equipment — equipment that was already producing sufficient fissile uranium to provide Germany with not just one, but several atomic bombs. The only obstacle was time.

'The pile we have built here,' Melzer explained, 'is a sphere, eight metres in diameter. It consists of no fewer than forty thousand graphite blocks, some of them containing uranium. The most active uranium, that is to say the metal, is at the centre of the pile, with the less active uranium oxide further out. Now, you see those rods there?'

He pointed towards three long bars projecting from the pile. 'Those are the safety controls,' Melzer said. 'They're made of wood, and to each of them we have fixed strips of a metal called cadmium. That's a kind of damper. It absorbs neutrons like a sponge absorbs water, and we can use them to shut down the atomic reaction if it shows signs of getting out of control. We can also use them to control the level of neutron activity while the reaction is taking place.'

Winter was beginning to grow accustomed to the new language of science. He pointed to some men in white overalls who were standing on top of the pile itself. 'Who are they? They look a bit apprehensive.'

Melzer smiled again. 'They have every right to be. We call them the "suicide squad". You see those big flasks in front of them? They're filled with a cadmium solution, and those men would break them to quench a runaway reaction.'

'What if that didn't work?' It was Warstiz who asked the question in a dubious tone of voice. 'What if the whole things does get out of hand?'

Melzer clapped him on the shoulder. 'We won't be here, and neither will Hechingen. But don't worry — you wouldn't know a thing about it,' he added cheerfully.

A scientist came up and spoke quietly into Melzer's ear, who nodded, and addressed the men on the platform.

'Gentleman, everything is ready. The experiment can begin. Please take your places.'

Otto Skorzeny looked across at Winter and Warsitz and beckoned them over to sit next to him. Melzer took a seat with several other scientists at a console that bore a cluster of dials and control switches. Winter wondered vaguely what they were about to see. Maybe the atomic pile would glow red, or something like that.

On the platform, there was complete silence. It was broken by a command from Melzer. 'Pull out Rod One.'

The first cadmium-plated rod was electronically controlled. As the assembled men watched, it slowly began to extend from the atomic pile. Somewhere a motor began to whirr, and a device on the console in front of Melzer began to emit a curious clicking sound.

For the next few minutes the scientists busied themselves with calculations, manipulating slide rules and monitoring needles that were tracing curves on graph paper. Then Melzer ordered the second rod to be pulled out.

Immediately, the clicking sound turned into a sharp rattle. Winter looked around, startled, but nobody else seemed to be alarmed. The knowledgeable Warsitz was gazing in fascination at the atomic pile. Winter gave him a nudge. 'What's happening now?' he wanted to know.

Warsitz glanced at him. 'The neutron production is increasing,' he said, 'The atomic fire is starting to kindle'.

Winter looked at the pile in perplexity. He couldn't see any sign of a fire. He was about to ask another question when he was interrupted by a further command from Melzer.

'Pull out the hand rod to three metres.'

A scientist who had been standing by the rod slowly began to extract it from the pile. The frantic rattling of the counter developed into a roar. Beside Melzer, a fellow scientist looked in sudden alarm at the needle on one of the dials. It was sweeping upwards rapidly.

'Don't worry,' Melzer said calmly. 'It will level off.'

It did. After a second or two the needle wavered and then stabilized. On Melzer's orders, the scientist beside the atomic pile continued to draw out the rod, a few inches at a time.

'Soon,' Melzer muttered. 'Soon it will happen.'

The rod came out another few inches. The roar from the instruments was almost deafening. The instruments on the console seemed to be going crazy. 'That's it!' Melzer exclaimed suddenly in triumph. 'The curve is exponential!'

'What did he say?' Winter asked. Warsitz smiled at him.

'He means that this time, the activity in the pile will not level off. The activity will go on doubling and redoubling. The pile is sustaining itself. A chain reaction is taking place.'

Winter looked at the pile again and gave a shrug. To him, it was all very disappointing. He had expected more than a noisy rattle from a few machines. For the next twenty minutes he sat there, his soldier's mind unable to grasp the reality of the atomic storm that raged in the heart of the device a few metres away.

The pile was heating up rapidly, and now radiation metres on the console were approaching danger levels. The pile was safe now, but in a few seconds it could become deadly.

'Insert the rods!' Melzer said urgently. As the rods slipped in, the noise from the counters diminished until it was reduced to a single regular click, repeated at intervals like the noise produced by a metronome.

Otto Skorzeny let out an explosive sigh and rose from his seat. He looked down at Winter and grinned. 'Well, what did you think of that? Not everyone is privileged to have a glimpse under the lid of Pandora's Box!'

Franz Warsitz smiled again. From the expression on Winter's face, he guessed that his superior had never heard of Pandora's Box. He would explain later.

At the console, Werner Melzer had also heard Skorzeny's words. He leaned back in his chair and stared dully at the instruments in front of him, lifeless now. In the excitement of the experiment, he had forgotten what the end product of all this effort was to be. Soon, he thought, Pandora's Box would burst wide open.

Unless he could do something, anything, to prevent such a catastrophe ...

Winter and Warsitz accompanied Skorzeny from the cavern. Outside, the air smelled good, carrying the scent of pines. He rolled saliva round his mouth. There was a curious dry, prickly sensation on his tongue. A sour taste, almost. It was probably something to do with the atmosphere in the cavern, he decided.

The two Brandenburg officers accompanied Skorzeny to the latter's staff car, saluted as he got in and watched him drive off, bound for his command post in the next valley. Winter glanced back at the place they had just left. The cavern's entrance was concealed by grey-green camouflage netting; you could pass within feet of it and still fail to notice that what resembled a piece of hillside was artificial.

This whole string of valleys was like that, Winter reflected. Every installation was camouflaged into near invisibility. Even the labour camp had been disguised to resemble a Black Forest village. The only features that still stood out were the electric pylons, carrying a steady flow of current to the industrial processes that were going on in Hechingen's mysterious underground factories.

Winter glanced up at the sky. Fleecy April clouds, scudding across the face of the sun before a stiff breeze, made it a day of alternate sunshine and shadow. So far, no Allied aircraft had put in an appearance; the machines, mostly American fighter-bombers, usually passed over two or three times a day, doubtless seeking targets of opportunity on the major roads leading from Ulm.

He looked at his watch and turned to Warsitz, commenting that it was time to eat. The mess hut that had been allocated for use by the Brandenburg detachment and the twenty-odd top scientists they were guarding was concealed in a small wood within easy walking distance of the laboratory complex that included the underground cavern they had just visited, and as they headed for it they were joined by Melzer, who ran to catch up with them. He caught Winter by the arm.

'Major,' he said in a low voice, 'may I speak to you in confidence?'

Winter nodded. 'Of course. Go right ahead.' He noticed that Melzer's brow was furrowed, as though with worry, and when the scientist spoke it was in a hesitant manner.

'How long do you think it will be, Major, before the Allies get here?'

Winter stopped in his tracks and looked at Melzer seriously. 'In some circles that would be called defeatist talk,' he said, 'and you must know the penalty for that. Be careful who overhears you.'

Melzer nodded. 'Yes, yes, I know. But you, Major-you are a rational man, and a front-line soldier. What's your opinion?'

Winter glanced round to make sure that no one other than Warsitz was listening, before he replied. 'The nearest Allied forces are less than fifty miles away. It depends on how long our troops can hold out in the Black Forest, but ... my own view is that the collapse will come quickly. The Allies could be here in a week, perhaps less. Why do you want to know? A day or two either way won't make much difference. They're coming here, and that's all there is to it.'

'A week,' Melzer muttered. 'A week ... that will be too late.' His face was almost ashen. He looked directly at Winter, and when he spoke again there was a hint of resolve in his voice.

'Major, I've got to stop this terrible, criminal thing. Will you help me?'

The Brandenburger was momentarily taken aback by the forthright question. He stared hard at Melzer. Long moments passed before he spoke.

Finally, he said: 'Look here, my friend. You yourself pointed out a few moments ago that I am a soldier. Therefore, I must do my duty, and my duty is to protect you and see that no harm comes to you. And when the end comes, as it will soon, I intend to see to it that you do not fall into the hands of the wrong Allies, you and your colleagues. What happens in between is no concern of mine.'

He poked a finger hard into the scientist's chest. 'But,' he said sternly, 'if you do anything foolish, anything likely to get you killed, then it *would* become a concern of mine. A very big concern. I might even have to place you under arrest, to keep you out of harm's way. Do you follow me?'

Melzer said nothing, just gazed at Winter and nodded dumbly. Winter grinned at the scientist's crestfallen appearance, and slapped him on the arm.

'Come on, Professor, don't be downhearted! Just think of all the money you are going to make, building lots of those contraptions of yours for the Amis. Now, come and have something to eat.'

Lunch consisted of vegetable soup, sausage and black bread. They made faces at it, but ate it nonetheless. Frugal though it might be, the food was better than the muck they'd been accustomed to eating on the Eastern Front.

They had barely finished when an ss orderly came in. He stood for a moment in the doorway, looking round, then spotted Winter and Warsitz. He strode over and clicked his heels, then bent down to whisper in Winter's ear.

Winter gave his companion a nudge. 'Come on, Franz. We've got to go to the command post. Just one moment.'

He rose and crossed the room to a table where some of his men were sitting, singling out his senior NCO, *Feldwebel* Ziska. The latter started to get up as Winter approached, but the officer indicated that he was to remain seated.

Quietly, Winter said: 'Wilhelm, there could be trouble. I don't know what sort of trouble, but until I get back make sure the scientists don't leave your sight. Most of them are working in the same place, so it shouldn't be difficult. And if any of these ss animals question your authority, remind them that we are acting on the direct orders of their own commander. Be gentle with them, though,' he added with a wink.

Ziska grinned broadly, revealing a large gap where his front teeth should have been. The butt of a Russian assault rifle had done that; the owner of the weapon had died in an extremely unpleasant manner, and Ziska had used the gun to good effect for some time until he had no longer been able to find supplies of the 7.62 mm ammunition it required.

'Don't worry, sir,' Ziska said, after swallowing a mouthful of sausage. 'I don't think they'll give us any trouble.' He said it with complete conviction.

Skorzeny's staff car was waiting to take Winter and Warsitz to the ss commander's trailer. On arrival, they found that two of his deputies were also present. Skorzeny came straight to the point.

'Gentleman, the situation is seriously deteriorating. The Russians have begun their offensive on the Oder. I have just received the latest reports by courier from Berlin.'

Winter had seen the little Storch communications aircraft land in a field earlier in the day. It was now parked under camouflage netting in a nearby wood. Winter did not envy the communication pilots; in their slow, defenceless aircraft they were at the mercy of the roving Allied fighters, and of necessity many of their missions had to be flown in daylight. Their only hope of salvation if they were attacked was to get down as quickly as possible, jump out and run for cover.

'I do not believe that our forces in the east can hold the Russians,' Skorzeny said frankly. 'They will probably be in Berlin inside two weeks. Vienna has already fallen.'

That piece of news came as a severe shock to Warsitz, who had relatives in the Austrian capital. The thought of Russian troops raping and looting in one of the world's most cultured cities made him feel physically sick. He strove to keep his face impassive and concentrated on what the *Sturmbannführer* was saying. There were further shocks in store.

'The American Seventh Army has entered Nuremberg,' Skorzeny went on. 'That too is sure to fall, leaving the Americans free to drive on to the Danube and Munich. In the north, the American Third Army has crossed the Elbe and is also preparing to drive forward to Berlin.'

Winter found himself considering the American capture of Nuremberg. At least, he thought, that puts the Amis between us and the Ivans. Good. One less thing to worry about.

'That is the general situation,' Skorzeny said, 'but there is something else. Two nights ago, according to a report I have just received, an enemy patrol consisting of about twenty men was observed in the vicinity of Sulz, a village to the south of Oberndorf. The patrol was seen by a sentry who was absent from his post without the proper authority. He did not challenge the patrol on the grounds that he was afraid for his own life and that of a girl who was with him. He has of course been shot.'

No one was much moved by that statement. In the hysteria and chaos that accompanied the collapse of the Third Reich, wholesale executions were commonplace. The slightest pretext sufficed.

'We think,' Skorzeny went on, 'that the presence of the enemy patrol deep inside our territory may be linked with the mysterious disappearance of a *Volkssturm* patrol in the hills a couple of days ago. That has not yet been confirmed. However, the important thing is this. If you draw a line on the map between the area where the *Volkssturm* patrol is thought to have vanished, and the village of Sulz, and project it a few miles further on, it ends up right here at Hechingen. The implication is quite clear, wouldn't you say, Winter?'

The latter nodded. 'It seems that Hechingen is the target,' he agreed. 'I'm surprised they've got as far as they have,' he said. 'The patrols in the Black Forest must be asleep, or badly overstretched. But surely our defences here are strong enough to stop them breaking in?'

Skorzeny looked at him with raised eyebrows. 'Oh, come along, Winter! You and I are both special forces' men; how often have your Brandenburgers moved freely inside enemy territory? I seem to recall the time when you led a hundred men into Russia and operated behind enemy lines for several weeks, against far more superior forces than we can muster. To lose twenty-odd trained men in mountainous, wooded terrain is the easiest thing in the world, as you well know.'

Winter had to admit that the ss officer was right. The fear, misery and sheer murderous brutality of that time in Russia, when he and his men had killed without thought or mercy, were still clear in his mind.

'I have sent out fighting patrols to sweep an arc to the west of Hechingen,' Skorzeny told him, 'and of course the *Volkssturm* are fully alerted. They will naturally fail to locate the British or American commandos, or whatever they are. So, the answer is to let them come. Let them make their move against us, and lose their element of surprise. Then we shall have them.'

'But what if they succeed in damaging the installations here before they are eliminated?' Winter wanted to know. 'Won't that be a significant setback to the project?'

Skorzeny gave one of his tight smiles. 'That is the point, Winter. It will make no difference. You see, it is too late. The Allies have already lost.' He indicated the two silent ss subordinates. 'Thanks to the encouragement of my colleagues here, our scientists have been spurred to great efforts.'

Winter wondered exactly what sort of encouragement had been applied, but said nothing.

'They have completed their task ahead of schedule,' Skorzeny said triumphantly. 'The first device is ready. Most of the components have already been flown to Norway, and the fissile warhead itself will be flown out tonight. Nothing can stop us now. Within forty-eight hours, New York will be in ruins.'

Winter had to work hard to convince himself that this was not some sort of bad dream. Skorzeny saw the expression on his face, and smiled again.

'So, Major, I can see that you need to be finally convinced. Well then, let us go and take a look at the proceedings, shall we?'

They left the trailer and climbed once more into Skorzeny's staff car, the two ss men getting into their own vehicle. The drivers followed a tortuous road through woodland, safe from the view of any prying reconnaissance aircraft, and descended into a valley that seemed quite unremarkable except for some shrubs that extended in unnaturally straight lines along the valley floor. Then, as the car drew closer, Winter and Warstiz saw that the shrubs were in fact carefully camouflaged landing lights, spaced at intervals along a lengthy expanse of levelled ground.

At the end of the valley, a huge awning of camouflage netting concealed the entrance to a hangar that had been dug out of the hillside. It opened directly on to the improvised runway. The cars came to a halt among some trees and their passengers descended. Skorzeny led the way into the hangar, striding purposefully ahead of the others. Armed ss guards who flanked the entrance, under the camouflage awning, saluted as the small party went past.

It was gloomy inside the hangar, but lights had been rigged up at strategic points around the Arado jet bomber that stood inside. Its bomb-bay doors were open, and a bulky object resembling a large oil-drum was positioned underneath on a trolley. A transparent hatch in the cockpit roof was open and the head and shoulders of a man rose through it as the newcomers approached. He levered himself up until he was sitting astride the fuselage behind the cockpit, then carefully descended to the ground by means of a series of hand-and foot-holds that were built into the side of the aircraft. He wore the uniform of a *Luftwaffe* officer.

He snapped to attention as Skorzeny came up, although his eyes swivelled in curiosity towards the two Brandenburg officers, who were strangers to him.

Skorzeny waved a hand. 'Relax,' he said. 'I have no wish to interrupt your work.' He turned to Winter and Warsitz and introduced the *Luftwaffe* pilot as Captain Rudolf Geischecke, then asked how the work was progressing.

'Very well, sir,' Geischecke told him. 'We are just about to start loading. The technicians are making a few final checks.'

He caught sight of Winter staring in what he believed was admiration at the Arado, and gave a broad grin although it did nothing to conceal the weariness that showed on his face.

'Beautiful, isn't she? She'll go up to eleven thousand metres and do eight hundred and fifty kilometres per hour, flat out.' He patted the side of the bomber's sleek fuselage, and his face assumed a sad expression.

'Tonight will probably be her last trip, though. Her engines are just about worn out. I've had to make a few high-speed runs up north lately, to avoid those infernal Mosquitoes.'

He looked at the canister underneath the bomb-bay. Ground crewmen were preparing to winch it up into place.

'Do you know what's inside that thing?' Winter asked conversationally.

The pilot looked at him in surprise.

'Of course I do,' he said, 'although I must admit I don't understand the workings of it entirely. What you are actually looking at is the casing that surrounds the warhead. It's very heavy because it's made of lead to stop dangerous rays of some sort escaping from the stuff inside. It's the biggest component I've had to carry so far, and the heaviest, so it's just as well this is going to be the last trip. It'll be all the old girl can do to lift that thing.'

'Well, Major,' Skorzeny interrupted. 'Now are you convinced?' Winter admitted that he was. Both he and Warsitz shook hands with the young pilot.

'I hope you make it,' the Brandenburg officer said. Geischecke gave a tired smile. 'Thanks, Major. So do I. Good luck to you, also. I don't

89

suppose we shall meet again.' He clicked his heels and gave a small bow, then turned back to supervise the loading of his aircraft.

Outside the hangar, the two ss men saluted Skorzeny and returned to their car.

Skorzeny watched them drive away and then turned to Winter and Warsitz. He regarded them thoughtfully for a few moments, then said: 'So, gentleman, our task here at Hechingen is almost over. But I have a further task in mind for you, one with a result that could be to our great advantage. My friends, I am about to take you completely into my confidence. Let us talk over there, among the trees, where there is no risk of being overheard.'

Winter and Warsitz followed Skorzeny into the shelter of the trees, glancing at one another in silent curiosity. After a few paces, the ss officer halted and faced his two companions, his brow furrowed. It was some moments before he spoke. When he did, they listened to his words with growing astonishment.

'When you first arrived here,' he told them, 'you must have seen my enthusiasm for this project. I sincerely believed that the bomb could still win the war for Germany. Since then, despite what I have said to you in the presence of others, I have lost faith. Germany is finished.' For a moment Skorzeny lifted his gaze to the patches of blue sky that were visible through the tree branches. Winter saw that his eyes were moist. Then the *Sturmbannführer* cleared his throat and recovered his composure.

'The reason for my change of heart is simple. Two days ago, I discovered that *Reichsführer* Himmler, the very man who ordered the ss to take control of the fission bomb project, has been attempting to enter into secret negotiations with the Allies — the western Allies, that is — to bring the war to an end before the Russians reach Berlin. There is another, more personal motive; in so doing he hopes to save his own neck. Whether he also hopes to save Hitler and other top Party men from the noose I cannot say. What I do know is this; the fission bomb has become Himmler's personal insurance. If the Allies will not agree to enter into separate peace negotiations by midnight tonight, Himmler will inform them that we have an operational bomb. If agreement has not been reached by the following night, he will order the mission against New York to proceed as planned.'

Winter took advantage of the pause to ask a question. It seemed an obvious one. 'But wouldn't that be for the best? There have been rumours that we have been trying to conclude a separate peace with the Americans and British for some time, so that we can turn on the Russians. Isn't that the only way to save Germany, at this late hour?'

Skorzeny laughed bitterly. 'No, my friend. I have thought long and hard over this matter during the past two days. A separate peace would only mean the extinction of many, many more young German lives in an attempt to throw the Russians from our territory — and personally, I don't believe that we could succeed in doing that. Far better to let Germany go under. She will rise again, one day.'

'Can't we stop this thing from happening?' Warsitz burst out. He nodded towards the hangar. 'It can't be difficult to sabotage the aeroplane, and —'

He stopped as Skorzeny raised a hand. The ss officer looked at him a little sadly. 'There's something you don't understand, Warsitz,' he said. 'The ss contingent here at Hechingen was picked by Himmler, not by me. There isn't a single man belonging to my Special Commando among it. I was brought in to keep order and to co-ordinate matters. I have no doubt at all that I am under surveillance, and that if I put a foot wrong He drew his index finger across his throat in a significant gesture.

Suddenly, what had seemed a mood of near despair lifted, and Skorzeny smiled.

'It took a great deal of behind-the-scenes string-pulling to get you and your men here,' he said. 'I'm well aware that you don't like the ss. I didn't care about that, because it was your fighting capabilities that I needed. Now things have changed, and your aversion to the ss might come in useful, especially if we have to fight our way out of here.'

Winter looked at Skorzeny and chose his words carefully.

'What exactly do you have in mind?' The implication behind the question was that he had reached a decision, and would go along with Skorzeny.

The latter also chose his words carefully. 'What I have in mind, Major, with the help of you and your men, is to establish contact with the Allied commandos and assist them to infiltrate the complex here. I shall personally brief them on where to find the Arado so that they can attack and destroy it. In that way the bomb will never leave Hechingen.'

Winter looked at him in astonishment. 'But that's impossible!' he protested. 'We've only got a few hours before dark, and we have no idea where the enemy commandos are.'

Skorzeny smiled at him. 'You're wrong, Major. I know exactly where they are. And so far, I am the only one who does.'

CHAPTER NINE

The ruins, centuries old, were still impressive. The crumbled walls had once soared in majesty above the secluded valley, their lustre reflected in the waters of a swift-flowing river. On the other side of the river, a smaller ruin, almost invisible under a dense coating of ivy that had hastened its collapse, was all that remained of a little chapel, the worship-place of the small army of serfs who had sustained the Benedictine abbey, their back-breaking effort fuelled by promises of rich rewards in a life to come.

The peasants had been the first to succumb when the Death descended upon them. It had come only days after a pedlar had passed through the valley, selling bales of wool. The Benedictine monks had slammed the great doors of their abbey shut and prayed for salvation, their ears closed to the pleas of the unfortunates outside who needed more than divine intervention; then they too had begun to die.

And soon the great abbey and its valley had become a place peopled only by ghosts, and over the centuries its great stones had toppled. The valley had become a brooding, untended place, visited by few, the home of ravens and other wild creatures, accessible only by way of overgrown tracks through the surrounding forest.

A small party of men moved rapidly along one of the tracks, following the contour of the slope as they headed towards the valley. It was led by Callum Douglas. Close behind came Joe McCoy, Liam Conolly and DeVine, who had never volunteered his first name during the entire mission. No one had bothered to ask him.

At the foot of the slope where the trees thinned out, the men paused and made a careful survey of the ground ahead before continuing. The ruins appeared to be deserted, but it would have needed a most expert eye to detect the men of Douglas's commando force in their concealed positions among the fallen stones.

Satisfied that there was no danger, Douglas led the others at a trot to the ruined abbey's toppled cloisters. He knew that his men would have their guns trained on the woods they had just left, in case they were being followed.

Sergeant-Major Brough came out of his hiding-place to meet them. His face was anxious, because they had been absent for longer than expected. Douglas was quick to reassure him.

'We didn't run into any trouble, Stan, and we've got a pretty good picture of what's up ahead.' He glanced at his watch. 'I think it will be safe enough to lie up here until it's dark. Bring the others in, will you? We might as well get the final briefing out of the way.'

The men were assembled within a couple of minutes. Brough posted look-outs at various points in the ruins, but within earshot, so that they too could hear what Douglas was about to say.

'You'll be glad to know that we are within two miles of the target area,' Douglas told them. 'From the top of the hill back there you can see the start of the valley where most of the action takes place, that's if our intelligence is correct. It seems as though it is, because there are some very suspicious gaps in the cultivated terraces that line the hillsides. It looks to me as though that's where they've buried their factories. There is also a main road running through the valley, with side roads that apparently lead nowhere. There was some traffic on the main road, but nothing out of the ordinary. Whoever is down there is obviously keeping out of sight.'

He paused and surveyed the faces around him, noting their weariness. He knew how they must be feeling. It was all he could do to stay on his own feet at times. He felt that he could sleep for a month. But sleep was something he mustn't think about. Not yet.

The one thing that really seems out of place,' he went on, 'is the fact that there are a lot of high-tension cables strung across the valley. They disappear into the trees. Now, we've been told that producing this super-bomb thing requires a lot of electricity, so that's obviously the key. If we destroy the electrical installations, we bring the process to a halt.'

That's if we aren't already too late, he thought grimly. He was aware that he was in a quandary, and was trying hard not to let his face show it. Here he was, within sight of Hechingen's mysterious installations, and he had no real idea what to attack in order to produce the best results. He had never gone into an operation with so little knowledge or target information, and he didn't like it.

Nor did he like what he saw in the eyes of his men. It could best be described as hopelessness. They were the eyes of men who had been waiting with increasing anticipation for the end of the war, and who were now being led into an operation that offered little prospect of survival.

*

Half a mile away, from a concealed vantage point behind some rocks on a hillside, a young man named Heinrich Treumann munched a fragment of sausage and kept an eye on the ruined abbey. Treumann had been out hunting at dawn, and it was purely by chance that he had sighted the commandos coming stealthily into the valley through the dawn mist.

Treumann had known exactly what he must do. His earlier instructions had been quite explicit. If he noticed anything untoward happening in the forests around Hechingen, anything at all, he was to report the fact to *Sturmbannführer* Otto Skorzeny — and to Skorzeny alone.

Treumann had served under Skorzeny since the beginning of the war, until that painful day nearly a year ago when a grenade fragment had removed his left eye during anti-partisan operations in Yugoslavia and caused him to be invalided out of the *Wehrmacht*. In January 1945, to his surprise, Skorzeny had suddenly got in touch with him and asked him to set about forming a network of resistance fighters called Werewolves in the southern area of the Black Forest. The idea was that they would wreak havoc behind enemy lines if the Allies crossed the Rhine and penetrated into Germany.

When Skorzeny had arrived at Hechingen, Treumann, armed with a pass that allowed him free movement in the restricted zone, had reported to the *Sturmbannführer* at regular intervals. It had been a routine and unrewarding assignment — until now.

The drone of an aero-engine attracted his attention. Looking towards the east, he saw the dragonfly-like silhouette of a Fieseler Storch rising above the hills. The aircraft cruised towards the valley and a couple of minutes later was circling overhead.

In the ruined abbey, Douglas and the others also heard the approaching aircraft and at once took cover. Douglas peered up at the circling Storch through a crack in the masonry. He was not unduly alarmed. It was probably just a routine local reconnaissance flight, he thought. Unless —

Unless the enemy knew that he and his men were there. Maybe they had known all along. He recalled the sirens they had heard just after they had crossed the Neckar. Perhaps they'd found those *Volkssturm* men, too. Even now, German patrols, summoned by the Storch, might be advancing on the valley. The temporary haven would become a deadly trap.

The Storch circled the valley twice, then turned into wind and began a steep descent from the eastern end, skimming above the densely clustered trees on the slope. Douglas saw that its big wing flaps were fully extended.

'It's coming in to land,' he exclaimed in surprise. 'Keep well out of sight, everybody. Safety catches on, and no shooting unless I say so.'

The Storch touched down on a water-meadow on the other side of the river, opposite the ruins, and came to a stop in an incredibly short distance. Its engine idled, the propeller continuing to revolve slowly. After a few moments two men got out and walked across the grass to the river bank. One of them was very tall and was wearing the black uniform of the ss; his companion, much shorter, wore a mottled camouflage suit of the kind used by German paratroops. His right arm was raised, and a piece of white rag fluttered from it.

The Germans came to a halt beside the river and faced the ruined abbey. The man with the white flag shouted something across the water.

Douglas turned to Liam Conolly. 'What's he saying?' he asked.

Conolly's face was a picture of astonishment. 'I don't believe this,' he muttered. 'They know who we are — or at least they've guessed — and they are offering to help us. They want to meet the officers face to face. I'm damned if I know what to think.'

'Well, they've got us cold, that's certain,' Douglas said. 'It would be easy enough to knock those two off, but the pilot of that aeroplane has still got his engine running, and he'd be off the ground and calling in the troops before we could get at him. We'd better do as they ask.' He looked at McCoy.

'Joe, you take command here. Liam, come with me.'

'Let me come too, Major,' said DeVine. 'I know who that tall guy is. Ever heard of Otto Skorzeny, the guy who rescued Mussolini?'

'Good God!' Through the crack in the stonework, Douglas stared at the tall man on the far bank of the river with a mixture of amazement, fascination and admiration. Skorzeny might be the enemy, but he was without doubt a very brave soldier.

'Let's get on with it, then.' Douglas rose and stepped out into the open, together with Conolly and DeVine. Over his shoulder, he said: 'Joe, if there's the slightest sign of trouble let those buggers have it. Don't worry about us.' 'Okay,' McCoy said. 'Good luck.'

The walk to the river bank seemed to last a very long time. The river itself was narrow, little more than a deep, fast-flowing stream, so that only a few feet separated the two parties. They stared at one another for a few moments. The German in the camouflage suit was the first to speak.

'I am Captain Warsitz,' he said in passable English, 'and this is Colonel Skorzeny.' Warsitz had decided to use the army rank, having failed to find a suitable literal translation of *Sturmbannführer*. 'The Colonel has a proposition to put before you. Do any of you have a knowledge of German?'

'No,' Douglas lied.

'Very well then, I shall translate,' Warsitz told them. He looked uncomfortable, but dropped into the role of Skorzeny's mouthpiece with surprising ease.

'Gentlemen,' Skorzeny said, 'I have reached the conclusion that the war is lost. Nothing can save us now, not even the secret weapon on which the *Führer* has placed such high hopes. Yes, gentleman, such a weapon does exist. It has come too late to save Germany, but it will be used nonetheless in a futile gesture of revenge that will only add to the misery and suffering of Germany's last days.' Briefly, he explained the nature of the bomb, and outlined the plans for its use. Beside Douglas, DeVine turned pale. His home was in New York.

Through Warsitz, Douglas asked the ss officer why he was unable to stop the mission from going ahead.

'The personal risk is too high,' Skorzeny admitted frankly. 'The ss guards at Hechingen are loyal only to *Reichsführer* Himmler. My only allies are the soldiers under the command of Captain Warsitz and his superior officer, and they are a mere handful. They have survived great hardships on the Russian Front; I have no wish to see them shot by their own countrymen.'

Inwardly, Franz Warsitz found himself marvelling at Skorzeny's complete about-face. Only a few hours earlier, he had spoken dispassionately about the execution of the young soldier who had first sighted the Allied commandos.

'What exactly are you suggesting?' Douglas wanted to know. Skorzeny looked at him gravely.

'What I am about to say has cost me a great deal of agonizing thought,' he said. 'I am not a traitor to my country, but neither am I stupid. When this war is over the Allies will divide Germany between them. The Russians may treat their Germans as a subject race, but the Americans and British will not. In time they will come to realize that the real enemy is in the east, and always has been. By that time the east will have reached the heart of Europe. So the British and Americans will make Germany strong again, and turn her into an ally. But if this weapon is used, the rebuilding of Germany will take a very long time, if indeed it takes place at all.'

He paused and coughed, hiding his mouth behind his hand, and waited until Warsitz had finished translating.

'What I am proposing,' Skorzeny continued, 'is to afford you and your men every possible assistance in penetrating the defences of Hechingen. Tonight, the sector of the perimeter closest to the place where the aircraft that will carry the bomb on the first stage of its journey is hidden will be patrolled by Captain Warsitz's soldiers. They will simply fail to see you as you slip through. Warsitz, the map.'

Warsitz, concentrating fiercely, inadvertently translated Skorzeny's last remark too, and flushed with embarrassment. He produced the folded map from his pocket and handed it to the ss officer. Skorzeny found a flat stone, inserted it carefully into the folds of the map, and threw it across the river. It landed at Conolly's feet and the Irishman picked it up.

'You will find all you need to know marked on there,' Skorzeny explained. 'The section of the perimeter through which you must pass, the location of the aircraft, everything. But you must carry out your task before midnight; that is when the aircraft is scheduled to take off.'

He looked at his watch. 'I must go,' he said. 'Well, do you agree to my plan?' His voice had taken on an impatient tone, which was admirably mimicked by Warsitz.

'Ask him about the scientists,' DeVine murmured. 'Ask him where they are.' Douglas did so, and Skorzeny frowned.

'I have my own plans for them,' he said firmly. 'I shall see that they are delivered safely to the Americans.'

Very shrewd, Douglas thought. Skorzeny obviously regarded the scientists as a kind of insurance policy. The man must have quite a few nasty skeletons in his cupboard; if he looked after the scientists and made sure they were handed over to the right people, maybe the Americans wouldn't string him up. They would probably give him a medal instead.

'One more thing,' Douglas said. 'If we go along with this crazy scheme, do we get any help in getting away afterwards?'

'That I can't promise,' Skorzeny told him. 'We can't let ourselves be seen to be giving you active assistance. But you will have the advantage of surprise — and anyway, you would not have had any help from us in the first place, would you?'

Douglas had to admit that that was so. He made up his mind. There was really no alternative now.

'Very well,' he said. 'We'll do it your way.'

The ss officer smiled across the water at him. 'Good!

And you need have no fear of treachery on my part. Whatever else I might be, I am a man of my word.'

And I am inclined to believe you, Douglas thought as he watched Skorzeny and Warsitz return to their aircraft. The Storch's engine roared and it bumped forward over the grass. The tail came up and it soared into the sky like a kite, turning steeply over the ruined abbey and then climbing hard to clear the slopes.

From his vantage point on one of them, Heinrich Treumann had viewed the proceedings in the valley with growing amazement. The actions of his former commanding officer completely perplexed him. He had seemed almost on friendly terms with the enemy; why, they had even saluted one another. It was all beyond his comprehension. Still, it was none of his business. He settled himself more comfortably on his perch and went on watching, as he had been told to do.

'Well, what do you make of that?' asked Douglas some minutes later, after he had related the recent events to an open-mouthed Joe McCoy. The latter was lost for words. At length, he managed to splutter:

'Jeez! Wake me up, somebody. You say that guy has actually given us a pass to go in there and blow the goddam place apart? It don't make sense.'

Suddenly, a thought crossed his mind. He frowned and turned to DeVine, who by this time was well known as the scientific brain of the party.

'If we blow up the airplane, won't that bomb inside it cook off and blast everybody to kingdom come?'

DeVine smiled tolerantly. 'No, Major, it will not. If what Skorzeny told us is true, the bomb is incomplete. The detonator is not present, only the fissile material, and without the detonator it will not explode.'

'Well,' Douglas commented, 'Skorzeny said that we have until midnight to do the job, so we'd better get cracking. Liam, let's have a look at that map.'

Conolly spread out the map on a flat tombstone and they clustered around it. Symbols had been drawn on it and annotated in English, presumably by Warsitz. The newly constructed airstrip used by the Arado jet bomber for its secret night excursions, Douglas saw, was in the valley adjacent to the one they had surveyed earlier; it lay about four miles away. The position of the underground hangar was clearly marked, as was the suggested route to be taken by Douglas and his men. Most of it passed through woodland. There were some roads to be crossed, but potential danger spots had been circled.

'Well, it doesn't look as though getting there is going to be a problem,' Douglas muttered. 'Getting out will be a different prospect. The logical move will be to go north, towards Stuttgart, and try to link up with the Allied forces. They can't be far away now.'

*

They were not, but the going had been much tougher than anyone had foreseen. With the Ruhr pocket now virtually annihilated, General Eisenhower had issued orders to General Jacob L. Devers, commanding the Sixth Army Group, to push south, taking Stuttgart and eliminating the German Nineteenth Army in the Black Forest. The us vi Corps, co-operating with French forces, was to envelop Stuttgart, seize lines of communication between the city and the Swiss border, and exploit the situation as far as the frontier to cut off the Germans in the Black Forest while the French liquidated them.

In some sectors the advance was relatively easy. In others, it was marked by savage fights that were less than battles, but more than skirmishes. On the right flank, the enemy reacted sharply to the 100th

Division's push towards Stuttgart, countering it savagely near Beilstein, twenty miles north of the city. In one instance, an infantry battalion approached a hill just north of Beilstein; forward elements crossed the wooded draw below the hill, climbed its exposed northern slope and reached the wooded crest, but the rest of the battalion was still climbing out of the draw when enemy mortars and artillery opened up on them, killing seventeen GIS and wounding over one hundred. When the battalion reached the crest, the Germans counter-attacked up the southern slope, suffering appalling casualties before they were finally driven off.

On the left flank, the 10th Armoured Division, after being delayed for some hours by steep hills and marshy valleys, suddenly made up for lost time by racing ahead for seventeen miles. Its leading echelons, smashing through road-blocks, pushed on and seized a bridge over the River Rems at Lorch, a few miles east of Stuttgart, driving into Lorch so swiftly that they captured the garrison — mostly bewildered *Volkssturm* — almost without a shot being fired.

As soon as the town was secure, several jeeps came in and parked in the town square, where the divisional commander had set up a temporary HQ. The jeeps carried a curious mixture of American and British personnel; there was even a Royal Navy commander. All were members of the Alsos Mission.

Colonel Boris Pash disembarked from the leading jeep and went in search of the divisional commander. The latter gave Pash a brief assessment of the latest combat situation. It was favourable; the Americans were making excellent progress and the 10th Armoured Division's next objective was Kirchheim, fifteen miles further south.

Two things disturbed Pash. The first was that French forces had already reached Reutlingen, which was only twenty miles from Hechingen. If the Americans suffered a serious setback, the French would be the first to reach the atomic research establishment.

The second was that there had been no word from Douglas. Pash had no way of knowing whether the commandos had succeeded in their mission — or whether they had been eliminated, and the world was about to explode in the faces of the so far victorious Allies.

*

In fact, Bill Mitchell had made several attempts to establish radio contact with Brigadier Master's HQ in Strasbourg, and all had failed.

There was nothing wrong with his radio set, and Strasbourg was well within its range, so he could only assume that the nature of the terrain was interfering with his radio signals. In the end, within sight of their target and with the radio just so much useless dead weight, he had abandoned it with Douglas's approval.

It was strange to be free of the bulky radio pack, Mitchell thought as he moved stealthily through the woods with the other commandos. After all, he had carried it on operations during most of his war, and it had become almost part of him. On one occasion it had saved his life, receiving a burst of bullets that had been intended for him.

Above the trees the sky was overcast, which pleased Douglas, for the moon had waxed considerably since they had begun their expedition several days earlier and was now prominent in the sky, its glow visible through the cloud cover. From time to time its full light shone through small breaks in the cloud, spreading dappled shadows on the ground; that, too, would help to disguise movement once Douglas and his men left the shelter of the woods.

*

In the small operations room adjacent to the underground hangar, Captain Rudolf Geischecke was also concerned with the weather, but for a different reason. Geischecke liked to stay down low on his clandestine missions to the north for two reasons: first because it helped his visual navigation, and second because at low altitude the RAF'S prowling Mosquitoes could not detect him with their airborne radar equipment. If the cloud descended to a dangerously low level he would be forced above it, and in the moonlight he would be a sitting target. In normal conditions he would have had sufficient speed to evade the night-fighters, but with the load he was carrying tonight he doubted that this would be the case.

For the third or fourth time he went out and looked up at the sky. The cloud *was* thickening and descending, there was no doubt about it, and the front it heralded was approaching from the north-west.

It was over four hundred miles to Flensburg, where he was scheduled to refuel before continuing to Trondheim, and he knew that if he delayed take-off until midnight, as planned, the front would beat him to it. Rudolf Geischecke therefore decided to bring forward his departure by forty-five minutes, and issued the appropriate instructions to his ground crew.

Anton, the Belgian, found himself shaking with fear as the commandos emerged from the screen of trees at the spot indicated on Skorzeny's map. Only the close proximity of the burly English sergeant, Brian Olds, prevented him from running back into the relative safety of the woods. Olds had been a tower of strength to the escapee, making sure he had plenty to eat, physically helping him over the patches where the going had been especially rough.

Anton was convinced that he was going to die, but at least he would die fighting, with a gun in his hand, and he was determined to take some of the hated enemy with him. Sometimes, he wondered what fate had befallen his two comrades, left far behind in the Black Forest; he hoped they would make it to safety. As for the others, still in the labour camp — well, he had no doubt what their eventual lot would be when their usefulness was at an end. Despite the peril, he counted himself fortunate.

Douglas had studied the route until it was indelibly etched upon his mind. Across the road, up the far slope in the shelter of the trees once more, over the crest and down into the valley. They would come out of the woods within sight of the hangar.

The tramp of boots echoed through the night and the commandos flattened themselves into the undergrowth at the edge of the wood as a German patrol tramped by. Almost immediately another appeared, marching in the opposite direction. Douglas waited until sufficient distance separated the two patrols, then gave the order to cross the road.

The commandos slipped over like shadows, crouching low, and made for the trees on the far slope. Olds seized a gasping Anton by the arm, helping him along.

Behind them, there were shouts in the night. Iron-shod boots echoed on the road again, coming at a run this time. Gunfire chattered and someone screamed, a harsh scream of shock and pain. There was no time to worry about that now. The commandos threw themselves into the shelter of the trees and kept on running. Bullets clipped twigs and leaves from the branches above them.

'Bastards!' McCoy gasped. 'Lousy bastards!' He was one step behind Douglas.

'Keep going,' Douglas panted. 'We've still got a job to do.'

On the slope leading up to the wood two men lay. One, an American, was dead. The other was Corporal Lambert. Moaning with the fire that burned in his shattered legs he slewed his body round to face the enemy troops that were charging towards him. With failing strength he pulled a grenade from his webbing and ripped out the pin with his teeth.

The grenade exploded with a sharp crack among the leading Germans. Some of them cried out and fell headlong. The others fired their machine-pistols, raking the slope at random, for they were unable to see the man who had thrown the grenade.

Lambert picked up his Sten gun from where it had fallen when he was hit and managed to sit up. Biting his lip against the pain, he cocked the weapon and opened fire, discharging the complete magazine at the shadowy figures who loomed over him, and had the satisfaction of seeing some of them crumple to the ground. His last gesture of defiance, before a burst of bullets took him in the chest, was to hurl the now useless gun in the face of the man who shot him.

Up among the trees, Anton gave a sudden yelp of agony and twisted from Olds's grasp. The sergeant stopped and grabbed his clothing, pulling him to his feet once more, but Anton screamed and cried out something in French.

'His ankle's gone,' DeVine shouted as he ran past. 'Leave him!'

Olds knew that he had no choice. Reaching down, he seized the Belgian's hand for a moment in his huge grip, then ran after the others.

Anton sat among the trees and slid a round into the breech of his Mauser carbine. It was strange, but he no longer felt any fear. The only emotion he felt was a craving for a cigarette. He would have liked a smoke, a decent smoke, before ...

Someone came crashing through the undergrowth, directly in front of him. He canted up the carbine and fired, taking only cursory aim. His bullet struck home and the figure tumbled like a shot rabbit. One, Anton thought with satisfaction.

Another shadowy figure came towards him, more stealthily, but Anton could clearly hear the noise of his passage through the undergrowth. He wedged his back against a tree trunk and waited, holding his breath.

A machine-pistol chattered, very loud, and slivers of wood sprayed from the tree trunk above the Belgian's head. He raised his carbine again and fired at the spot where he had seen the muzzle flash of the enemy weapon. There was a crashing, rolling sound, accompanied by a dreadful shrieking. Two, thought Anton.

There was no time to force another round into the breech. The enemy were coming at him from all sides now. His bullet-riddled body slumped lifeless at the foot of the tree, cradled by the roots.

The commandos heard the loud rattle of gunfire as they plunged on up the slope. Douglas did not yet know who had been left behind, but whoever it was had bought time for them in holding up the pursuit.

If only we can finish what we came to do, was the thought that hammered over and over through his head. Lower branches whipped at his face as he ran and he sensed that blood was mingled with the sweat that poured down his cheeks. His lungs heaved as they sucked in air.

Then suddenly he was over the crest, almost falling headlong as he slid down the opposite slope, the muscles of his legs taut and aching as he braced himself. The others were still with him, gasping for breath in the darkness. He smashed into a tree trunk, bruising his shoulder painfully, and gave a loud curse.

Suddenly, he was conscious of a strange noise in the night — a sound like the whistling of a steam kettle. It grew in crescendo, puzzling him. He had heard nothing like it before.

There was something else. As he approached the bottom of the slope and the trees began to thin out, he saw lights glowing dimly in the darkness. Suddenly, he understood the significance of the curious noise. He managed to take an extra-deep breath and yelled:

'Come on — faster! The plane's taking off!'

Suddenly he was out of the trees, and able to see what lay ahead. The first thing that entered his field of vision was the jet bomber itself, its sleek lines illuminated by the lights of the improvised flarepath. The shrill note of its engines continued to rise as the pilot opened the throttles to full power.

Douglas, summoning all his energy, ran towards the Arado as it began to move, firing his Sten. The others were opening fire too, the louder thump of the Americans' Thompson guns mingled with the lighter rattle of the British weapons.

The Arado gathered speed. Douglas felt the hot wash of its jet exhaust and smelled the curious stench of the engine fuel, rather like burning paraffin. The bomber was well clear of the running men now, racing between the lights on either side of the airstrip. He saw its nose lift and suddenly it was airborne, its engines thundering now as it clawed for altitude.

There was no time to dwell on the sick sense of failure that threatened to overwhelm him. Heavy fire was coming at his men from the edge of the wood they had just left, and from a hillside to the right of it where the hangar must be located. He was sharply conscious of the fact that he and his men were silhouetted against the lights of the flarepath.

'Get over to the other side of the runway!' he shouted. 'We've got to find some cover!'

If they could hold off the opposition by fighting a series of rearguard actions until they reached the shelter of the woods on the other side of the valley, they might be able to split up into small groups and make their way northwards. Some, at least, would stand a chance of joining up with the advancing Allies.

About a hundred yards on the far side of the airstrip there was a shallow dip in the ground. They fell into it more or less by accident and lay prone. McCoy slid into place beside Douglas and gave him a nudge.

'Well, Cal,' he said, 'it was nice knowing you.'

'It's not over yet,' Douglas told him. 'We'll give the bastards a run for their money.'

Flares arced up from the far side of the airstrip and burst into brilliant light overhead, drifting down under their small parachutes. It was a mistake on the part of the Germans, who had not realized that the commandos had taken cover. The flares served only to illuminate the Germans themselves as they came forward in short dashes.

Funny, Douglas thought as the enemy came on. They always attack in the same manner. He fired methodically, only when a clear target presented itself, conscious that his ammunition would not last for ever. What was it Wellington had said at Waterloo, or somewhere? They came on in the same old way, and we stopped them in the same old way. Something like that.

'Oh, Jesus,' McCoy said quietly, looking to the left. 'Here comes the cavalry.'

Douglas looked too, as he fitted a fresh magazine to his Sten, and his heart sank. Some vehicles were coming round the side of the hill at considerable speed, their headlights full on. He heard the rattle of tracks.

Tanks, maybe? No, he decided, half-tracks. Either way, it didn't make much difference.

He opened his mouth, about to order his men to make a run for it, knowing as he did so that they would never reach the far side of the valley. It was then that the incredible happened.

The leading vehicle opened fire — not on the spot where the British and Americans were concealed, but on the attacking Germans.

CHAPTER TEN

The commandos watched in astonishment as glowing strings of shells from quick-firing 20-mm cannon impacted among the advancing enemy troops, scything them down like corn. The second half-track, whose gun was of a heavier calibre, turned it towards the entrance to the underground hangar and also opened fire. There was a flash of light and a terrific thud as the shells found their mark among some drums of aviation fuel. A great balloon of flame burst from the hangar. Men ran from it screaming, their bodies on fire.

The flames pouring from the mouth of the devastated hangar illuminated the airstrip. The silhouettes of the four vehicles were clearly visible now; Douglas was able to identify the leading pair as Kfz 7/2 half-tracks, one carrying a four-barrelled 20-mm *Flakvierling* and the other a single-barrelled 37-mm anti-aircraft gun. Both weapons were deadly against ground targets.

The two vehicles bringing up the rear were Opel trucks. One of them veered towards the commandos' position. Douglas ordered his men to hold their fire.

The truck stopped some distance away and a figure jumped down. The man ran forward, gesticulating in the light of the flames.

'Come quickly,' he called out in English. 'Get into the truck!'

'Come on!' Douglas shouted. 'Do as he says!' He recognized Warsitz's voice.

The commandos ran to the trucks and scrambled aboard. Hands reached down to help them. Someone grabbed the burly Olds by the collar and hauled him into the vehicle as though he weighed no more than a rag doll. *Feldwebel* Ziska grinned toothlessly down at him.

'Hello, Tommy,' the Brandenburger said.

'How do, Fritz,' Olds grunted, pulling himself up into a sitting position beside the German.

Douglas climbed into the cab beside Warsitz, who was driving. The truck lurched into motion in the wake of the two half-tracks. There was no longer any shooting; the troops who had been guarding the airstrip lay scattered on the ground, all except for a handful who had managed to retreat into the woods.

The small convoy moved rapidly along the airstrip and eventually reached a road that ran in a north-south direction at the eastern end of the valley. Douglas allowed Warsitz to concentrate on his driving for a while, then his curiosity could no longer contain itself.

'What happened, for God's sake?' he demanded to know.

'Soon after we returned to Hechingen after our meeting with you, an urgent signal arrived for Skorzeny,' Warsitz told him. 'He was very shaken. The signal, which was from *Reichsführer* Himmler, ordered him to fly to Munich immediately and organize a last-ditch defence in the Bavarian Mountains. The officer who received the signal was one of the men planted by Himmler himself, so Skorzeny had no choice but to obey.'

It was beginning to drizzle, and Warsitz set the truck's windscreen wipers in motion.

'At the time we didn't think it would make much difference to our plan,' he went on. 'Then, after Skorzeny had flown out, we suddenly found ourselves surrounded by a group of ss. There was no point in resisting for we were heavily outnumbered. They relieved us of our weapons and locked us in a building, along with the top scientists. We heard one of them remark that we were all to be shot on Himmler's orders and the installations at Hechingen destroyed to prevent their secrets from falling into the hands of the Allies. The scientists were of no further use now that their task had been completed, and we — well, we knew too much about the whole business.'

Above the sound of the Opel's engine, Douglas heard Warsitz chuckle.

'Those swine forgot that we are Brandenburgers,' he said. 'They underestimated us. They left only a couple of their men to guard the building where we were held captive. They were disposed of very quickly, after we broke out.'

He glanced at his companion. 'Do you happen to have any English cigarettes, Major?' he asked, rather hesitantly. Douglas nodded and produced a crumpled packet of Players from his battledress pocket. He found his lighter and lit two cigarettes, one of which he passed to the driver. Warsitz took a deep drag and exhaled the smoke slowly through his nostrils. He gave a loud sigh of pleasure.

'*Wunderschön*,' he said gratefully. 'You can't imagine how it feels to taste good tobacco. But, to continue. We knew that we couldn't hope to take on the whole of the ss contingent at Hechingen. We needed some help. Fortunately, the place where we had been imprisoned was not far from the forced labour camp. We killed the guards there, broke into the armoury and released the prisoners. It was about this time that we heard the sound of firing in the distance, and realized that you must have run into trouble.'

Douglas marvelled at Warsitz's matter-of-fact tone. He was beginning to appreciate what tough, disciplined fighters these Brandenburgers must be, not unlike the Special Air Service itself.

He was unaware that he had fought them before, in both North Africa and Yugoslavia.

'The prisoners agreed to cause as much trouble for the ss as possible before making a run for the forest,' Warsitz explained. 'For our part, we seized whatever weapons we could find and overpowered the crews of those two antiaircraft vehicles. We also commandeered the two trucks, loaded the scientists into one of them and some of our men into the other, and set off to see if we could assist you. It seems we arrived just in time.'

'In time to save our skins, yes,' Douglas said, 'and we're grateful to you for that. But we didn't stop the jet bomber. It must have taken off early. Incidentally, where is your own commanding officer?'

'On the leading half-track,' Warsitz told him. 'You will meet him in due course. He is a very fine soldier. It is regrettable about the Arado. It will be well on its way by now. But there may still be something we can do to stop the final mission — if we can reach the Allies in time.'

*

The cockpit of the Arado was almost silent, except for the whisper of the slipstream flowing past the glazed nose. The noise of its engines trailed behind it in its wake as the jet bomber scudded along just below the lowering cloud base.

Geischecke was not aware that the aircraft had been fired on at the Hechingen airstrip. At the time, he had been intent on starting his take-off run, and the sound of the jet engines had drowned the noise of the shooting.

As the bomber flew on, following a course that was almost due north, Geischecke gazed sadly down at the wreckage of his homeland, visible in

110

the flames that licked at the ruins of cities. He passed over ruined Hanover, where sporadic bursts of anti-aircraft fire from Allied gun batteries lanced up at him; as always the gunners misjudged the speed of the Arado and the shells burst behind the aircraft.

The British had not yet reached Hamburg. As Geischecke approached the city he saw that it was under air attack, searchlights were probing the sky and he could see the flash of bomb-bursts. He had no fuel to spare for a detour, so he would have to take a chance and fly straight through the middle of the air-raid.

The beams of the searchlights reflected uselessly from the base of the clouds. The British night bombers must be bombing blindly with the aid of their radar. He increased his speed as much as he dared, anxious to be clear of the area as quickly as possible. The smoke of the burning port entered the Arado's cockpit, invading his face mask and stinging his nostrils.

Then the savage flak and the searchlights were behind him, and he breathed a sigh of relief as the Arado sped on over what, for the time being, was still German-held territory.

It would have been the ultimate irony if, at this crucial stage of the operation, he had been shot down by his own side.

The flat plain of Schleswig-Holstein unrolled beneath him. His instruments were now picking up Flensburg's homing beacon. He called up the airfield and gave his call sign. A terse voice answered him, asking for positive identification by means of a certain code. Geischecke gave a satisfactory reply and a few minutes later he saw the flarepath spring to life in the distance ahead of him.

He brought the jet bomber expertly down to land and taxied towards the refuelling point. In the bomber's belly, the cargo of deadly atoms slumbered. It was almost exactly an hour since he had taken off, and in that time he had flown the length of Germany.

*

It seemed to Douglas that the convoy had been doubling back on its original course, twisting and turning along precipitous roads in the darkness. He questioned Warsitz about it, and the Brandenburg officer explained that they were following a semi-circular course that was designed to take them clear of towns such as Tailfingen, where there were known to be German garrisons.

Shortly before dawn, the vehicles pulled off the road and took shelter in a narrow ravine, which was almost completely hidden by trees. Their occupants climbed down and stretched their legs gratefully.

Warsitz brought Helmut Winter over to meet the British and American officers. He noticed that the NCOS and men were already making cautious attempts to get to know one another, the Americans and British handing out cigarettes. It should have felt very strange, to be fraternizing with the enemy like this in the heart of his own country, but somehow it did not.

Suddenly, Winter knew that these men were no longer the enemy. They had too much in common. The uniforms might be different; the attitude and bearing were the same. He reached out and shook hands in turn with Douglas, McCoy, Conolly and DeVine. With the aid of the German speakers in the Allied party, they managed to strike up a conversation. Warsitz found himself smiling; he remembered Douglas's earlier denial that any of his men spoke German. A cautious man, he thought, and very shrewd.

'This is as far as we dare take the vehicles,' Winter told them. 'From now on we shall begin to encounter increasing numbers of German troops; the nearest fighting, as I understand it, is only fifteen kilometres to the north.'

His face took on a grave aspect. 'We have helped you so far,' he said, 'and we shall continue to help you. If we meet trouble we shall even fight alongside you — provided the opposition consists of the ss. I will not fight against ordinary *Wehrmacht* troops. Therefore, we must proceed very carefully on foot, taking care that we are not discovered by my own people, until we are in a position to contact yours.' Conolly indicated the scientists, who were huddled together and speaking in hushed voices to one another. 'Are they fit enough to undertake a forced march across country?' he asked.

'They will have to be,' Winter replied simply. 'I must admit, however, that some of them do not appear to be very well.'

DeVine looked at him. There was a curious expression in the American's eyes, as though he had just realized a very important fact. He excused himself and went over to the group of scientists. They looked at him a little apprehensively as he approached, and muttered amongst themselves.

'Which ones among you do not feel well?' DeVine asked abruptly. Three of the scientists raised their hands hesitantly, followed by a fourth. The American beckoned to this man and asked him to step forward. He had red blotches on his face.

'Let me see your arms,' DeVine demanded. After a moment's indecision the scientist rolled back his right sleeve, then his left. Both arms were red and swollen.

'Now remove your hat,' the American ordered. He inspected the man's head carefully and stepped back, nodding. 'Just as I thought,' he muttered, and inspected each of the other men in turn. None showed the same symptoms as the first man, but they were pale and there were dark shadows under their eyes.

'You don't understand, sir,' one of the men said in a voice that quavered.

'On the contrary,' DeVine told him. 'I understand only too well.' He strode off to rejoin Douglas and the other officers. Douglas asked him what was wrong.

'Some of those men are suffering from the effects of radiation,' the American told him. 'They have been exposed to a radioactive source for prolonged periods without proper protection. To put it simply, harmful rays have passed into their bodies. We still know very little about the effects of radiation, even though the man who discovered radioactivity around the turn of the century, Henri Becquerel, developed sore spots on his body. He was in the habit of carrying a radioactive source such as uranium salts around with him in his waistcoat pocket.'

'So, what's to be done?' Douglas wanted to know.

DeVine shrugged. 'Get them to proper medical attention as quickly as possible,' he said. 'One seems to be worse than the others.' He pointed the man out.

'Okay,' Joe McCoy said. He turned and sought out his master sergeant. 'Walecki!' he roared. 'Detail some men to take care of those sick guys, will you? They'll have to carry 'em, if necessary.'

'Sure thing, Major.' Walecki picked out three Rangers and assigned them to the task.

With Warsitz interpreting, Winter explained the route he proposed taking to Douglas, pointing out features on his map. The route wound its way through the Swabian Jura Mountains, with heights rising to three thousand feet. It was going to be tough on the scientists.

'It is the only way,' Winter explained. 'We must at all costs avoid the valleys. There, do you see? We make a start there. We must climb.' He pointed to a peak that loomed to the north-east of their present position.

Douglas looked at the sky. The drizzle had stopped and the clouds had lifted. Already there were breaks in them. Soon it would be broad daylight, and he was conscious of one danger. With the Allied spearheads apparently only a few miles away and the weather breaking, the sky would soon be swarming with fighter-bombers sweeping ahead of the American forces. They needed to get to the wooded mountain slopes as quickly as possible. Hungry though he was, he dismissed all thought of breakfast and shouldered his pack. With Winter keeping pace alongside he strode purposefully along the ravine towards the first objective, glancing back briefly at the crocodile of men forming up behind. He had started off with twenty under his command; now he had more than sixty, including Winter's troops.

They had been walking for six hours, with frequent halts, before they reached the summit of the first hill, two thousand eight hundred feet above sea level, or so Douglas's map of the area informed him. The scientists seemed to be utterly exhausted, with one or two exceptions, and Douglas decided to call an hour's rest. They would all benefit from something in their stomachs.

The British and Americans shared out the last of their rations with the Germans. *Feldwebel* Ziska looked doubtfully at the slice of bully beef Olds handed to him.

'Go on,' the former Norfolk farmer's boy urged him. 'Go on, get stuck in. It's good.' He made eating motions.

Ziska took a cautious bite, chewed and nodded appreciatively. Then he raised a finger, as though struck by a sudden thought. He delved into a pocket and produced a piece of sausage, which he handed to Olds. The burly sergeant gazed at it. It was coated in fluff from Ziska's pocket, and indefinable black shreds clung to it. He brushed them off and popped the fragment into his mouth, eyes bulging as he tried desperately to chew and swallow it as quickly as possible while at the same time holding his breath to stifle the pungent odour of garlic that emanated from it. Ziska grinned at him and ate the rest of his bully beef with obvious relish.

Conolly went and sat beside Helmut Winter, who glanced sideways at him and went on eating. After a few moments, Conolly asked: 'Major, why are you doing this? Helping us, I mean.'

Winter's brow furrowed. At length, he said, i have been asking myself that question. The whole idea was Skorzeny's, not mine, and he was prompted by the actions of Himmler. After Skorzeny left Hechingen — well, my men and I could easily have escaped.'

'But you didn't,' Conolly pointed out. instead, you risked your lives to help us out of a tight spot.'

Winter stared directly into the Irishman's eyes. Slowly, he said: 'My men risked their lives because they followed my orders, as they have always done. As for me ...' He paused, as though searching inwardly for the right words to use.

'I have seen terrible things in my time, Captain. In Russia, for example. When we first invaded we were greeted as liberators by the people of the Ukraine and elsewhere. We sincerely believed that we were embarking on a kind of crusade against the greatest evil the world has ever known. Liberators. Can you believe that?'

Conolly nodded. 'I suppose so. Please go on.'

Winter's face took on a grim expression. 'After the frontline troops came the ss extermination squads. They murdered men, women and children. The taint spread to the whole *Wehrmacht*. It drove the Russians who had hailed us as liberators to hate us. It drove us to hate, too, when we saw what the ss were doing. We would kill ss men in Russia whenever the opportunity arose, Captain, and took far greater satisfaction in it than we did in killing Russians.'

He sighed and poked at the ground with a twig. 'The ss,' he said, 'always the ss. They have cut the throat of the German fighting soldier, perhaps of the whole German race. There are terrible rumours about death camps all over the territories we occupied. And the tragedy is that when the war is over, and the truth finally emerges, no one will believe that the ordinary German soldier never knew about such matters, or had a hand in them.'

He threw the twig to the ground in a gesture of disgust and stood up. Conolly rose too and turned to face him. Winter shook his head despairingly.

'And even now, even at this late hour, the ss are still committing atrocities, still pushing forward with their plans for senseless destruction. Pandora's Box,' he added.

Conolly was startled. 'What?'

Winter shook his head again. 'Nothing. It was just something that Warsitz explained to me. It doesn't matter. If only — '

He stopped speaking abruptly as a drum-roll of sound echoed over the countryside. Both men knew it for what it was.

'Artillery barrage,' Conolly announced. 'Come on, let's take a look.'

They hurried to the summit of the hill and crouched down, gazing out over the terrain that lay to the north. After a moment they were joined by Douglas and McCoy. The view from the summit was unparalleled, the land unfolding like a map. Smoke was rising from various points on the horizon, and the explosions of the artillery barrage continued unchecked.

'Ours or theirs?' McCoy asked.

'Both,' Douglas told him. 'More ours than theirs, though.' He swept the horizon with his binoculars, then consulted his map. 'That smoke over there seems to be coming from Reutlingen,' he said, 'but whatever lies a few miles to the left of the town seems to be taking quite a pasting.' He looked at his map again. 'I'd say that was Meizingen.'

McCoy also inspected the map, and traced a line with his index finger between their present location and the spot Douglas had just mentioned.

'Hell,' he muttered, 'that's close. Less than eight miles, at a rough estimate. I guess we needn't go looking for the front line, Cal. It's coming to us, and fast.'

McCoy was right, although he would not learn the details until later. French and American armies had bypassed Stuttgart, effectively sealing the town's fate, and were within a few miles of joining forces. The Germans were left with only one escape corridor which was being pressed hard from both sides.

'Yes. Well, I think it might be a good idea to stay put for a while. Take a look at that.'

He handed McCoy his binoculars and pointed northwards, to where high ground enclosed a long valley. A twisting road ran the length of the valley, passing a couple of miles to the west of where Douglas and the others were encamped.

McCoy looked, and gave a sharp exclamation. What had been a dark, indistinct blur at the northern end of the valley resolved itself, through the glasses, into a slowly moving mass of men and equipment. There was no cohesion, no orderliness in the movement. Some of the groups of men stuck to the road, others swarmed along the adjacent hillsides.

As the column drew closer, Douglas saw that it contained very few motor vehicles; most of the transport was horsedrawn. This must, he thought, represent only one small corner of the whole picture, because at his estimation the column comprised fewer than two thousand men, but he knew what he was seeing: these were the dregs of a defeated army, its reserves of fuel and ammunition exhausted.

Beside him, Helmut Winter kept looking up at the sky. The clouds were broken now, and large patches of blue showed between the cumulus as it scudded before a stiff north-westerly breeze. It could only be a matter of time, Winter thought, before the inevitable happened.

The fighter-bombers came less than an hour later, just as the leading elements of the column drew abreast of Douglas's vantage-point. Stan Brough saw them first, a cluster of silvery dots spreading low over the hilltops, their wings momentarily lit by a flash of sunlight. It was as though the absence of camouflage on the aircraft underlined the fact that the Allies had complete mastery of the sky.

The men in the valley did not see the fighter-bombers until the aircraft were upon them. The machines — fat-bellied P-47 Thunderbolts — attacked in pairs, flying wingtip to wingtip. No anti-aircraft fire opposed them as they roared the full length of the valley, strafing with their machine-guns. Belatedly the men scattered, desperately seeking cover like a colony of ants sprayed with boiling water. The Germans watched the spectacle with grim faces, and Douglas spotted one or two of them casting malevolent looks towards the Americans. Winter spotted it too, and spoke sharply to the men involved, his voice rising above the roar of the aero-engines.

The Thunderbolts made two passes and then climbed away, heading back in the direction from which they had come. After a few minutes the straggling German column resumed its southward march. Dozens of bodies were dragged from the roadway and left to lie on either side.

One of the scientists broke down and sobbed uncontrollably, head pillowed on his arms, his shoulders heaving. Melzer put an arm around him and spoke soothingly to him.

The ordeal of the retreating German troops was not yet over. Another wave of fighter-bombers skimmed along the valley, strange-looking machines of a type Douglas had never seen before. McCoy told him that they were Airacobras, aircraft which the Americans had used against the Japanese early in the Pacific War. These too attacked in pairs, dropping small bombs from under their wings and then returning to make a series of strafing runs. One of them flew low overhead, and Douglas saw that instead of white American stars its wings carried blue, white and red roundels, the red being the outer circle. The fighter-bomber belonged to a Free French squadron.

At last the scream of engines faded away. The battered enemy column had passed out of sight now, leaving its dead sprawled in the valley. Silence returned, and for a long time no one on the hill spoke a word.

Douglas looked to the north again through his binoculars. He found no sign of life and movement, except for the smoke that drifted distantly across the horizon. At length, he turned to Winter.

'I don't think there's anything in front of us now but Allied troops,' he said, with Conolly interpreting. 'The choice is yours. Either you can continue with us, or you can go south, after your comrades.'

Winter's grey eyes regarded him thoughtfully. 'Give me a few moments,' he said, and assembled his men around him while he spoke to them. His message was clear and simple.

'The English major has given us an alternative. Either we go on with him, and surrender to the Allies, or we make our way south. We have been together a long time; I will not make any decision until I know how you all feel.'

There was a long silence, and Winter was acutely aware of the scrutiny to which he was being subjected. Finally, after what seemed an interminable length of time, *Feldwebel* Ziska spat through the gap in his teeth.

'Aah, what the hell. It's all done for, anyway. If we go south we'll probably run into those ss bastards again, or get ourselves killed by some shitty little lieutenant wanting to make a glorious last stand and go to Valhalla. I say we go along with the Tommy major.'

Winter looked at his NCO with great affection, and heard the general murmur of approval. It was the response he had hoped for. He turned on his heel and strode back to where Douglas was waiting. Winter was carrying a machine-pistol; he now offered it to the ss officer in a gesture of surrender.

Douglas smiled at him and said something Winter did not comprehend. He looked questioningly at Conolly.

'Major Douglas says thank you, but he has a gun of his own. When he wants yours, he'll ask for it.' They all laughed, and any tension that might have existed quickly evaporated.

A few minutes later the party resumed its trek, descending down the steep slope into the valley far below. Because of the condition of the scientists progress was slow; it took them a long time to cover a couple of miles, and Douglas was aware that time was one commodity of which he was desperately short. Making contact with the Allies was one thing. Finding someone who would believe his incredible story was quite another. He had the scientists, of course, and Winter's men, so someone was bound to sit up and take notice. But valuable time would be wasted while they were interrogated, and there would also be delays while he got a signal through to the Strasbourg HQ. By the time he had got all the formalities out of the way it would be too late, and the aircraft carrying the fission bomb would be on its way to New York. He had already done sufficient mental arithmetic to be aware that, because of the time difference, the bomber could complete the whole of the outward flight in darkness. It would only face the sunrise on the homeward run — if there was a homeward run. By then, it would no longer matter.

A tap on the shoulder interrupted his thoughts. McCoy pointed along the valley. There was a broad grin on his face. 'Looks like we've got company,' the American said.

Douglas looked. From the cover of some woods in the distance, tanks were moving out on to the roadway. They were American Shermans.

CHAPTER ELEVEN

On Douglas's orders the Germans, soldiers and civilians alike, placed their hands on their heads in a gesture of surrender, the British and Americans having finally relieved them of their weapons. Douglas, standing some distance apart from the others, stood in the middle of the road and watched the tanks as they approached.

The leading Sherman ground to a halt a few yards away. In the turret, a helmeted soldier kept a point-five machine-gun trained on the group in the roadway. Beside him, the tank commander leaned forward, his hands on the rim of the turret hatch, and stared at Douglas in perplexity.

'Who the hell are you?' he asked.

'Major Douglas, British Special Air Service,' Douglas told him crisply. 'And this is Major McCoy of the United States Rangers. We've been on a special mission, and these men are our prisoners.' He indicated the Germans.

The Americans looked at them. 'Civilians. What do you want with civilian prisoners?'

'They are scientists,' Douglas explained patiently. 'They've been engaged in top secret research work, and our orders were to bring them out.'

'And the others?'

'Their guards. They're okay. In fact, they helped us to get out. Without them we'd have had it.'

'Where have you come from?' the tank commander wanted to know. Douglas told him.

'Hechingen!' the American exclaimed. 'Why, that's where we're heading. Our orders are to get there with all speed and hold the place until some brass hats arrive. Have you seen much opposition on your travels?'

'There's a German column some distance down the road,' Douglas told him, 'but it's been under air attack and has taken a beating. As far as we could make out it consists of under two thousand men, very badly disorganized and with no heavy weapons. They'll probably head for the woods as soon as they see you coming.'

Captain DeVine came to stand alongside Douglas. He looked up at the tank commander. 'You mentioned some brass hats who were making for Hechingen,' he commented. 'Do you know where they are?'

The American nodded. 'Sure. They're about two miles back, towards the rear of the column. They've been moving forward with us for days. Keep on going back that way and you'll run into them. Look out for the jeeps flying the pennants. Gotta get going now.'

He tipped a finger to his helmet by way of a salute and waved his arm in a forwards motion. Douglas and the others moved to the side of the road as the Sherman surged forward, its tracks kicking up a spray of stone chippings.

'Better get off the road altogether,' Douglas said. 'We don't want any of our men falling under one of those things.'

Stan Brough came up, looking concerned. 'Sir,' he said, 'that scientist — the one who looks really sick. He's started throwing up, and can barely stand. I don't think he's in any shape to go on.'

Douglas pondered for a moment. 'All right, Stan. I'll go on ahead with Major McCoy and Captain DeVine. You stay here with the rest and keep an eye on our Germans. I don't think they'll give any trouble. There won't be any language problem — Liam and their Captain What's-his-name will see to that. We'll send some transport back for you as soon as we can.'

Douglas told Conolly what he intended to do, then set off with McCoy and DeVine, keeping to the rough ground by the side of the road as the procession of Shermans rolled past. All but the leading tanks had infantrymen clinging to their hulls. Some of them shouted and waved at the three officers, but most looked utterly weary.

The three men walked on rapidly, perspiring now in warm sunshine. Douglas glanced at DeVine; the American had acquitted himself well, despite Douglas's early misgivings about him.

Devine was the first to spot the jeeps. They were drawn up some distance off the road, beside a farmhouse, and were guarded by a small posse of American military policemen. They pointed their carbines at the three officers as the latter made their approach.

'I guess I'd better handle this, Cal,' said Joe McCoy. Douglas, eyeing the MPS, made no objection.

'Now just you hold it right there, sirs,' one of the MPS called out. 'Let's have some identification.'

'Major McCoy, us Rangers.'

'Okay, sir. You come forward. You others, stay put.'

McCoy advanced and confronted the MP, hands on hips as he spoke. Douglas and DeVine, who could overhear snippets of the conversation, gathered that the policeman wanted to see McCoy's identity documents, which the American, in common with the other members of Douglas's group, was not carrying for security reasons. Douglas sensed that McCoy was beginning to lose his temper, and was about to intervene when a voice was heard from the farmhouse. There was no mistaking its authority.

'I know these officers, Sergeant. Allow them to pass.'

The tall figure of Colonel Boris Pash stood framed in the doorway of the farmhouse. He beckoned to them to enter as the MP stepped aside.

The farmhouse kitchen was occupied by a group of men, all officers, who were busily munching their rations. Several bottles of wine stood on the table. The officers looked up with interest as Pash entered with the three newcomers.

Pash picked up an already-opened bottle and handed it to McCoy. 'Spoils of war,' he grunted. 'Pass it round. I guess you could do with it.'

He made some brief introductions, then turned to Douglas. 'What happened?' he asked simply.

Douglas provided him with a short resume of their mission, including their escape from Hechingen with the scientists and the German soldiers. 'Which reminds me,' he added. 'They're sitting a mile or two down the road under guard. Some of the scientists are pretty sick. They need transport.'

Pash gestured to one of his officers, a us Army captain. 'See to it, John, will you?'

The man rose. 'Right away, sir. I'll get on the jeep radio. There are some supply trucks in the woods a few hundred yards back.' He left the room quickly.

'So,' Pash said, 'all our fears are confirmed. They do have the bomb, and it's now apparently in Norway. Do you know where, Major?'

'According to Major Winter, the German officer, the base for the mission against New York is Trondheim. He also said — or rather,

Skorzeny said — that whether the mission is flown or not depends on whether our side agrees to some demands from Himmler. Something about a separate armistice, leaving what's left of the German armies to turn on the Russians.'

'We know about those,' Pash told him. 'We are in constant touch with Strasbourg, and we've been kept informed. We knew that this notion of a separate armistice was in some way linked with the atomic bomb project. We also know that all such demands have been rejected out of hand, not just by the Supreme Commander, but by Prime Minister Churchill and President Truman.'

'President *who*? The question, uttered in astonishment, came simultaneously from three mouths.

Pash looked at each man in turn. 'Of course,' he said slowly, with a hint of sadness in his voice, 'there was no way that you could have known. You've been absent for a week. Gentlemen, it is my sad task to tell you that President Roosevelt died suddenly on the twelfth of April, the day your mission began.'

They were stunned. 'Jesus Christ,' McCoy whispered, and sat down heavily in a nearby chair. DeVine had turned pale. Douglas looked from one to the other. He wondered how he would have felt if someone had just broken the news to him that it was Winston Churchill who had died, and not Roosevelt, at the very hour of Allied victory. Shock and sadness, certainly — but open grief? He began to realize how special a place Franklin Delano Roosevelt had occupied in the hearts of the American people, and it was a revelation to him.

The heavy silence was broken by the officer to whom Pash had referred as John, who returned with the news that transport was on its way to pick up the commandos and their captives.

'Very well,' Pash said. 'We'll get the scientists back to Strasbourg as quickly as possible once we've had a preliminary look at them and then fly them out to England. The German troops will be sent to a prison cage after they have been interrogated. We shall push on as planned to Hechingen, but first of all I have to get a signal to London. We'll catch that German bomber on the ground at Trondheim,' he added confidently, 'and knock it out before it has a chance to take off.'

'What about our men?' Douglas asked.

'I suggest you wait for them by the roadside,' Pash told him. 'You can travel to Strasbourg with the scientists, and from there to England. There are people who are going to be very interested indeed in your report on this mission.'

The three of them went out into the sunlight, McCoy still clutching the bottle of wine. By the time the transport returned with their men and the Germans, they had finished the drink and were feeling considerably more light-hearted than had been the case earlier.

The American trucks halted in response to McCoy's upraised hand. The SAS men and the Rangers were in the leading vehicle, the scientists in the one behind and Winter's soldiers, under heavy guard, in the truck bringing up the rear.

Douglas said a quiet word to McCoy, who went to the truck containing the German soldiers. He spoke to the MP in charge. The man looked dubiously at him, then said: 'Well, if you're giving me an order, I guess that's okay. But make it quick, sir.'

He gestured to Winter and Warsitz, who climbed down over the tailboard. Douglas looked at Warsitz and said, 'I know your major does not speak English, so perhaps you will convey my words to him. I wish to thank you very deeply for what you did, and I only wish that we might have met in happier circumstances. You and your men will be well treated in prison camp, and if there is ever anything we can do for you in return — well, you know what I mean,' he concluded lamely.

Warsitz looked at him and smiled. 'I understand, sir. Good fortune to you. Good fortune to us all.'

He drew himself up and saluted. Winter followed suit. Douglas and McCoy returned the compliment, then reached out and shook hands with each man in turn. The gesture did not go unnoticed by the MP in charge.

'Hey, gentlemen,' he called out, 'that ain't allowed. That's fraternization!'

McCoy stared up at him. 'Go shit in your hat, soldier,' he said quietly.

Royal Air Force Station Banff, Scotland. 18 April 1945. 18.00 hours GMT.

The airfield at Banff, on the shores of the Moray Firth, was a desolate place, little more than a network of runways and a cluster of Nissen huts. But since the summer of 1944, the RAF Coastal Command squadrons based there, operating rocket-firing Beaufighters and Mosquitoes, had probably inflicted more losses on enemy shipping than any other units of their kind. The pilots who flew them were a cosmopolitan gathering; as well as men from every corner of the British Empire they included Norwegians and Frenchmen. They and their navigators were skilled at seeking out and destroying in the North Sea area, particularly in the treacherous fjords of the craggy Norwegian coast.

By this stage of the war most German shipping was concentrated between Denmark and Norway, and in the past fortnight there had been some dramatic actions in which enemy vessels had been literally blasted apart by rocket salvoes. The tally had included three u-Boats.

On this day, the crews of the Banff Strike Wing's squadrons had been briefed to make a dusk attack on a force of German minesweepers which had been sighted off southern Norway. It had therefore come as a complete surprise when, at the last minute, a priority signal had been flashed to the airfield's operations room ordering a change of target. One of the pilots, a veteran squadron leader, winced when he heard what it was at the briefing.

'Trondheim,' he muttered to his navigator. 'Bloody hell! I heard the Huns had been moving all sorts into that place lately — extending the main runway, too. Loads of flak, I'll bet,' he added mournfully.

Forty-five Mosquitoes were assigned to the mission. They were to attack the airfield's installations with rockets and cannon, and in particular were to ensure the destruction of any large four-engined aircraft that was located, either on the ground or in the air. The weather would be marginal, with a bank of fog rolling down from the Arctic Circle. It was going to be a hell of a trip, the squadron leader thought. Still, they all were. One more wouldn't make much difference.

The Mosquitoes, as usual, were to be escorted by three squadrons of long-range Mustang fighters, flown mostly by Polish pilots, from Peterhead. The Germans still had plenty of Focke-Wulf 190 fighters in Norway, and they could be troublesome. On one occasion in recent weeks, the 190s had shot down nine Beaufighters from a neighbouring strike wing at Dallachy.

Laden with rockets and fuel, the Mosquitoes took off and set course, keeping low over the sea. Their crews would not see land again for nearly six hundred miles.

The weather grew steadily worse as they flew on, with grey tendrils of cloud reaching down almost to the surface of the water. Rain squalls lashed down, rivulets streaming over the windscreens of the speeding aircraft.

In the middle aircraft of the first wave, the wing commander glanced anxiously at the chronometer on his instrument panel. They should have made rendezvous with the Mustangs several minutes ago, but there was still no sign of the fighters. In this murk, it would be little wonder if the two formations missed one another.

The Mosquitoes flew steadily on over the icy, foam-streaked sea, lost in a grey-green world of cloud and water that grew steadily darker with every passing mile.

*

Twilight of a similar kind had also descended over Trondheim, but at this higher latitude it was deeper and more oppressive. In another couple of hours it would be pitch dark.

The preparations were almost complete. The components of the bomb had been assembled under the direction of the scientifically trained ss officers, and the massive device, nearly twenty feet long, was secured inside the Junkers 390's bomb bay. An access ladder led from the bay up into the main fuselage; after the bomber had climbed to its cruising altitude one of the ss technicians accompanying the mission would climb down and arm the weapon by setting a barometric fuse. When the bomb was released its fall would be retarded by a parachute, giving the aircraft a chance to escape the explosion, which would occur when the bomb descended to an altitude of five hundred feet over its target.

This, the scientists had calculated, would produce far more damage from blast and heat than if the weapon detonated on the surface. But no one could be certain; indeed, no one even knew whether the weapon would work at all.

In the underground operations bunker, Hermann Kreipe and his crew were putting the finishing touches to their flight plan. None of the airmen, including Kreipe, knew what sort of weapon they were to drop on New York; only the ss officers flying on the mission knew that. Kreipe had not even been allowed to see the bomb, although he knew how much it weighed — necessary information in order to calculate such factors as take-off weight and fuel consumption.

One thing Kreipe did know, and had known for some time. With a five-ton load in the bomb bay, they would not have enough fuel to get home. He had pointed this fact out to the ss officer in charge of the operation at Trondheim. That problem, the man said, had been taken care of. Kreipe was to fly the Junkers to an exact spot over the Atlantic, where the crew would bale out and be picked up by a u-Boat.

'I don't believe a damn word of it, Gerhard,' Kreipe confided later to his navigator. 'I don't doubt that with your first-rate navigation we could rendezvous with a submarine all right; it's just that I don't believe there *is* a submarine, and in any case baling out into the North Atlantic at this time of the year isn't my idea of salvation.'

'To my mind the whole damn thing is crazy, anyway,' the navigator said. 'Why don't we just tell them to stuff it, and refuse to fly?'

'Because they'll shoot us, Gerhard, that's why. We've got to go ahead with this mission, because at least that way we'll have some slender chance of saving our own skins. Those ss thugs seem hell-bent on committing suicide; well then, let them. We'll complete the mission, and bale out over dry land. Pass the word quietly among the rest of the crew. We'll work out some sort of scheme just before take-off.'

'That's not going to be easy, either,' Gerhard pointed out. 'I've just had a look at the weather. It's clamping down fast. You can't see the far side of the airfield as it is.'

'As long as I can see the flarepath we'll get off all right,' Kreipe told him. 'Once we get above the muck we'll be fine. If Iceland is fogbound we won't have to worry about patrolling night-fighters. We'll have the sky to ourselves, Gerhard.'

*

Out over the sea, the Mosquitoes flew on in semi-darkness. The wing commander could no longer see the other aircraft in the formation. Fog streamed past the Mosquito's wings. Beside him, the navigator, a New Zealander with several thousand hours of flying experience behind him, sweated with the mental stress of keeping the aircraft on an accurate heading.

There was danger just ahead, danger in the towering black crags of the Norwegian coast.

'Landfall in one minute, skipper,' the navigator said. The wing commander gave a curse.

'This is bloody well impossible! Can't see a thing. The whole coastline is clamped solid. We'll never — Christ!'

Over on the right a sudden ball of fire glowed in the fog. Showers of sparks cascaded from it, then were extinguished. A Mosquito and its crew had just slammed into the cliffs, to be instantly obliterated in a mighty explosion of fuel and rocket warheads.

Reacting instantly, the wing commander hauled back the control column, at the same time yelling a warning to the rest of the formation over the radio. The Mosquito practically stood on its tail as the pilot took it skywards at full throttle. A few seconds later it burst out of the fog bank into a clear sky. A crystal cold night was falling over the Norwegian Sea, and the stars were gleaming. The land to the east was invisible, enveloped under an unbroken blanket of fog and cloud.

The wing commander radioed the other Mosquitoes, aborting the mission. As he turned the nose of his aircraft back towards Scotland a cold fury gripped him at the thought of the two lives that had been lost. Maybe others would die, too, as the aircraft groped their way down to land over the Scottish coast. And all because of a senseless bloody order to carry out an airfield attack in conditions such as these. He beat his gloved fist against the instrument panel in impotent rage, and swore to have someone's scalp — if he was lucky enough to get down in one piece.

*

The crew were in their positions, waiting tensely for the moment they were all dreading — all except Kreipe, who would be too busy controlling the heavily laden Junkers on take-off to worry about anything. On the earlier proving flight across the Atlantic the aircraft had carried a double crew; this time, there was no need of that.

Kreipe could not see the runway ahead. To assist him in the take-off, he had ordered vehicles to be positioned on either side of the runway with their headlights on. The lights showed up as dim circles in the fog, but they would enable him to keep the huge bomber on a straight path. The nearest lights were reflected from the whirling propeller blades as Kreipe slowly opened up the six engines to maximum power.

The Junkers shuddered as he kept the brakes on. Steady now, he told himself, not just yet. Wait until you feel her straining at the leash, and then — brakes off!

The bomber lurched forward, gathering speed in the darkness. Sitting in one of the vehicles by the runway, Captain Rudolf Geischecke watched it thunder past, dimly visible as its bulk cut a swathe through the fog, and wished he was on board. His Arado had seen its part of the mission through faithfully, but it would never fly again. For what remained of the war he would be earthbound at this remote outpost.

Kreipe grasped the control wheel firmly. He did not need to look at his instruments to gauge the bomber's speed. Another set of lights flashed past and he eased the wheel forward, lifting the tail. Just a few more seconds ... a slight backward pressure on the wheel, and the rumbling of the undercarriage ceased. They were airborne. The BMW radial engines roared healthily as the bomber climbed steadily through the fog. The sighs of relief from the crew were audible over the intercom.

'The course for Point Alpha is two five zero degrees magnetic, Captain,' the navigator said.

Point Alpha, where Gerhard would fix the bomber's position exactly, was a featureless spot in the ocean one hundred and fifty miles to the south of Iceland.

CHAPTER TWELVE

In the USAAF Officers' Club at Reykjavik, Iceland, a game of poker had been in progress pretty well continuously for two days. There were plenty of people to keep it going, because several crews on passage between the United States and Britain via the Icelandic route had found themselves weatherbound. The aircrews on their way to Europe did not mind this in the least, and prayed fervently that the bad weather would last until the end of the war. For the crews travelling in the opposite direction at the end of their tour of duty, and anxious to be home, it was a different matter.

Most were bomber crews, but there was one exception. Captain Joshua T. Martin and his navigator, Lieutenant N.M.I. Whiteman (The N.M.I. was Whiteman's idea of a joke, and stood for No Middle Initial) were the crew of a P-61 Black Widow night-fighter. For several months following the D-Day landings of June 1944 they had roved the night skies of Europe along with the rest of their squadron, sharing the night intruder task with the Mosquitoes of the RAF, but in recent weeks, with targets becoming increasingly difficult to find, the squadron had been released from combat duty.

The remainder of the squadron had set off from Iceland three days earlier, but Martin and Whiteman had been forced to stay behind when their Black Widow developed mechanical trouble. By the time it was fixed the weather had clamped down, and so far it showed no sign of lifting. Now, after what amounted to a two-day binge, Martin and Whiteman were beginning to show signs of wear and tear. Moreover, they were beginning to run out of money.

The ringing of the telephone roused the barman, who had been dozing on his stool. He lifted the receiver and listened, then called across the bar to Martin, who muttered 'What the hell!' and laid his cards face down as he rose to answer the summons.

A minute later he returned and beckoned to Whiteman. His face was ashen. 'Earl,' he said, 'you ain't going to believe this. We've been ordered to fly.'

*

The Northrop P-61 Black Widow was a formidable fighting machine, and was the first American aircraft developed specifically for night-fighting. A large and heavy aircraft, it was easily as big as an average medium bomber and packed a tremendous punch, being armed with four 20-mm cannon and four .50 machine-guns. Its two Pratt and Whitney Double Wasp radial engines developed 2,250 horsepower each, and gave it a top speed of 360 miles an hour.

The heart of the Black Widow was its SCR-720 radar set, which was installed in a second cockpit above and behind the pilot's. Whiteman, feeling far from well, busied himself at it now, warming it up and checking that it was functioning correctly. In front of him, Martin was carrying out his engine checks. Normally, a third crew member, the gunner, would have occupied the transparent nacelle at the rear of the fuselage, between the twin tail booms, but together with the squadron's other gunners he had returned to the State on board a transport aircraft.

Whiteman completed his checks and called the pilot over the intercom. 'Skip, just what the hell is going on here? Look outside — you can't even see the goddam wingtips.'

'Yeah. Look, Earl, I've told you all I know. We've gotta launch off and shoot down some Kraut airplane that's going to be passing south of Iceland shortly. That's it. Why, I don't know. Maybe it's carrying some of the Nazi hierarchy, or something like that. The commanding general was pretty explicit, though. We've got to consider ourselves expendable, old buddy.'

Shit, thought Whiteman. And we were going home.

The voice of the Reykjavik controller interrupted his thoughts. 'Two-five, scramble, scramble. We have radar contact with bandit, two zero zero miles south-south-east of Iceland. Altitude is sixteen thousand feet.'

'Roger.' Martin opened the throttles and looked ahead along the runway. The flarepath was dimly visible. This was going to be hairy. Okay, concentrate on the directional gyro to keep straight.

Streams of condensation whirled back from the propeller tips as the Black Widow surged forward. Martin kept one eye on the direction indicator and the other on the dimly visible runway lights. The Black Widow seemed to be glued to the runway.

Momentary panic gripped Martin as a wave of fog obscured the light ahead. The aircraft seemed to be careering into a black void. Heart in mouth, he pulled back the control column and literally tore the Black Widow off the ground.

'Two-five airborne,' he said over the radio. His voice was a harsh croak.

'Roger, two-five, steer one-nine-zero to intercept.'

The Black Widow bounded up through the swirling vapour and popped like a cork from a bottle into the starlit realm high above. Martin turned on to the heading the controller had passed to him. From now on, the radar at Reykjavik would pass constant directions to him, sending the Black Widow on a course which, some one hundred and fifty miles out over the freezing waters of the North Atlantic, would converge with that of the mysterious enemy aircraft.

On the outward flight, Martin had plenty of time to ask himself how he was going to land back at Reykjavik once his mission was over. His brain came up with no answers.

*

The Junkers droned steadily on. The roar of its six big radial engines had long since merged to produce a kind of dull, heavy silence in the cabin. The bomber was flying on automatic pilot, and Kreipe was already starting to feel the effects of boredom. Looking down, he could see nothing but an unbroken layer of cloud, stretching from horizon to horizon. Up above, the stars were clearly visible, though, enabling Gerhard to keep an accurate running fix of the aircraft's position by means of astro shots.

Seated behind the pilot, one of the ss officers on board glanced at the luminous dial of his wrist-watch and smiled in satisfaction. It was well past midnight. Today was the twentieth of April — the *Führer's* birthday. What a present this would make for him! The timing of the operation was impeccable.

*

'Two-five, target range is ten miles, crossing you port to starboard. Turn right five degrees.'

Martin acknowledged and moved the control column, varying the course slightly in accordance with the controller's instructions.

'Any joy yet, Earl?' he asked. The navigator-radar observer peered at his fluorescent scope and twiddled the controls of his radar set.

'No, nothing yet,' he grunted. The seconds ticked by and the Black Widow sped across the sky, eating up the miles between it and the target aircraft. Control had said that the target was flying at sixteen thousand feet, so Martin stayed at eighteen thousand; in that way he hoped to obtain a good sighting of the enemy machine as it was silhouetted against the cloud tops.

'Still nothing,' Whiteman muttered. 'No, wait — CONTACT! Christ, it's big!'

A large, firm, luminous blip came into view on the cathode ray tube.

'Gently starboard and go down. Range five miles.'

Martin manoeuvred the Black Widow as instructed, at the same time informing Reykjavik that they were in radar contact with the hostile aircraft. Whiteman kept his eyes glued to the radar scope.

'Keep turning gently starboard and level out,' he said over the intercom. 'Range two and a half miles. Steady now. Range two miles. We're coming in nicely. Where do you want him?'

'Keep him starboard and above. About ten degrees starboard. What range now?'

'Just over a mile. Throttle back a bit. Can you see anything yet?'

Martin peered ahead through the windscreen. 'No, I ... Hold on. There's something — God almighty! I've never seen *anything* that big! It's okay, Earl, I've got a good visual.'

Every nerve in his body was tense as the huge bulk of the Junkers filled the sky ahead. It was only a few hundred yards distant.

All hell broke loose as he pressed the gun button and the Black Widow's eight guns banged and clattered. Streams of tracer converged on the Junkers, and the American fighter's cockpit filled with the acrid smoke and smell of cordite.

*

The first burst of cannon shells and machine-gun bullets smashed into the Junkers' rear fuselage, killing four of the crew outright. The rear gunner, unhurt, came to his senses and opened fire on what he thought was the silhouette of an aircraft. Most of his shots went wide, but some found their mark in the Black Widow's port wing. Martin cursed and kicked the rudder, slewing the aircraft away from the danger.

'All right then, you bastard!' he said out loud. He straightened the aircraft and pressed the gun button again. The explosion of his cannon shells danced and sparkled across three of the Junkers' six engines. The American fighter was within two hundred feet of the target now. Martin continued firing in short bursts, and saw a red glow appear between two of the bomber's engines. Moments later a ribbon of vivid white flame burst from the trailing edge of the wing as the explosive shells ignited fuel from a ruptured tank. The flames spread rapidly until the whole of the wing's centre-section was ablaze.

In the Junkers' cockpit, Kreipe screamed over the intercom to the bomb-aimer. 'Get up front and jettison that damned bomb! I might have to ditch, if she'll hold together long enough!'

The bomb-aimer clawed his way forward to the nose compartment, pushing past the two ss men. Both had heard Kreipe's shout.

'No!' one of them yelled. He drew his revolver and fired two shots into the bomb-aimer's back. The man fell forward into the nose section, his dying hand scrabbling for the bomb release lever. He found it and pulled.

Freed of its restraining shackles, the heavy weapon dropped clear and slammed into the unopened bomb doors with a tremendous crash, ripping them clear of the aircraft. One of them, caught by the slipstream, whirled sharply upwards and removed one of the bomber's twin tail fins.

Astern of the crippled Junkers, Martin veered sharply away to avoid the big object that fell from the bomb bay. Fragments of the bomb doors and tail whipped past the Black Widow, dangerously close.

The huge bomber was finished. As Martin watched, its burning wing began to break up. He dropped further astern to watch the terrifying spectacle.

Suddenly, the wing broke clear of the fuselage and disintegrated in a shower of blazing fragments. The rest of the bomber nosed down and went into a ponderous spin, its rotation increasing as it plummeted towards the cloud layer below. He knew that no one would be able to get out, and thought that perhaps it was just as well. Better a quick death for the crew, than a slow one in the icy water.

He called up Reykjavik with the news that the bomber had been destroyed.

The excited voice of the controller came back over the radio. 'Great show, Two-five! Come on home, now.' Martin was already on his way. 'Just one small matter,' he radioed. 'How the hell am I going to get down?'

'Boy,' the controller said, 'don't you worry about that. We'll bring you right over the base here, and you are authorized to bale out. We'll be ready for you.'

'Hell,' said Whiteman mournfully from the rear cockpit, 'I don't trust anyone. We bale out of a serviceable airplane, and they'll probably dock the cost of the goddam thing off our pay.'

*

The bomb, still unarmed, drifted down through the swirling vapour, accompanied by fragments of glowing wreckage. It cleaved into the water and continued its descent, still dragging its retarding parachute. It fell for six thousand feet, its strong casing resisting the enormous pressures to which it was subjected.

Finally, it dug its way into the soft mud of the ocean floor, and as the weeks and months went by the silt, stirred by eddies and currents, gradually covered it.

Unlike the evil regime that had created it, the atoms at its core would live for a thousand years.

EPILOGUE

Although men were still fighting and dying in the Far East, Callum Douglas's war in Europe had been over for three months now. But still the nightmares came, and he knew that it would be a long time before the terrors and hardships that had created them passed from his subconscious mind.

This one was different. He came awake slowly and uneasily, not with the usual panic-stricken jolt. Worms crawled in his mind, and it was as though the darkness around him was filled with the whisperings of thousands of newly dead.

He switched on the bedside lamp and sat up. Beside him his wife, Colette, stirred in her sleep and half-turned towards him. She stretched out a hand; he took it and stroked it tenderly.

'Hush, now,' he whispered. 'It's nothing. I'm just going to make myself a drink.'

He rose, pulled on his dressing-gown and went downstairs to the library, where he poured himself a stiff measure of whisky from his father's drinks cabinet. He sat down in a leather armchair and took a sip, rolling it around his tongue before swallowing. It helped to dispel the bad taste in his mouth.

They had gone to bed early that night, before nine o'clock, tired after a day's walking in the Perthshire hills. Douglas had fallen asleep immediately, but it had not lasted. He looked at the clock on the library wall; it was not yet half past ten.

On the other side of the world it was morning. A lone Superfortress, destined now to become the most famous aircraft in history, droned steadily south-eastwards to its base at Tinian, in the Marianas.

Behind it, a mushroom cloud rose over Hiroshima.

Printed in Great Britain
by Amazon